NUNCHUCK CITY!

BRIAN ASMAN

A MUTATED MEDIA PRODUCTION

Edited by Max Booth III

Cover Art by Matthew Revert

Interior Layout by Lori Michelle
www.TheAuthorsAlley.com

Also by Brian Asman

I'm Not Even Supposed to be Here Today
(Eraserhead Press)
Jailbroke

Coming Soon

Comic Cons
Man, Fuck This House

For Steve James, the real-life inspiration for every Chuck Norris joke there ever was

ARE YOU TIRED OF GETTING YOUR ASS KICKED? ARE YOU CONSTANTLY GETTING BEAT UP AT SCHOOL, THE OFFICE, YOUR CHURCH?

Well, come on down to Hawk Dragon Martial Arts where we'll teach you how to fly like a hawk AND a dragon! With the combined might of two of nature's deadliest predators, and under the tutelage of ninth-degree karate black belt Skip Baxter, the Most Dangerous Man in Turbo City and inventor of the highly deadly Bax-Do fighting system, you'll be vanquishing your enemies in no time! Bullies? Armed robbers? Stan from accounting? Put a foot up ALL their asses, and more!

I'M SKIP BAXTER, AND I APPROVE THIS MESSAGE. OSHIRIGAKUSAI!

KICK IT

SKIP BAXTER, the Most Dangerous Man in Turbo City, gently guided his cherry-red '89 'Vette into the strip mall parking lot, paying more attention to the incredibly photogenic and more importantly lethal-as-fuck hands resting on the steering wheel than the road. He'd been down to the police station no less than three times to register them as Deadly Weapons™ but never got past the desk sergeant, a tall woman with a laugh like a twat-tickled donkey. Hell, once he even showed up at a gun buy-back in the parking lot of the long-shuttered Niederman Toys building, even brought his own bone saw, but all they did was laugh at him.

Bunch of pansies, with their Glocks and their nightsticks and their pussy-ass radios to call for backup, Skip thought. *I'm Skip Baxter, and I'm my own goddamn backup.*

Skip eased into the reserved space with SENSEI emblazoned on the asphalt in front of Hawk Dragon Martial Arts, the dojo he'd founded two years before, and got out, the scent of baking conchas from the panaderia next door thick in the air. Idly, one of his Deadly Weapons™ wandered down to the thick roll of fat straining the elastic waistband of his tracksuit.

1

He gazed at the OPEN sign on the panaderia door for a hot second before remembering he was supposed to be doing that stupid keto diet. Marsha swore by it, she'd dropped seven pounds. His complexion was already going south, a bright sheen of grease covering his face, clogging his pores. But he had to do *something*. Middle age was a real motherfucker.

At least he still had his hair. Thick, black, lustrous, cut in an exaggerated mullet hanging down between his shoulder blades, held back with a hachimaka embellished with the Hawk Dragon logo—a hawk, with dragon claws and shit, breathing fire. Totally badass.

Just like Skip.

Skip fumbled through his key ring until he found the front door key, nodding his head in time to the soft ranchero music leaking out of the bakery. He shoved the key in the lock and turned it, but the key didn't want to go. He turned it back the other way.

Locking the door.

Skip frowned. He must have forgotten to lock up the night before. No surprise, that one little wiener kid, what was his name, Robert or Mark maybe, failed to stand the requisite ten fucking feet back while Skip was demonstrating a roundhouse kick. What followed was a shitload of crying—heavily frowned upon at Hawk Dragon Martial Arts—and the realization that little Robert or Mark's nose looked slightly different than when he trotted through the front door at the beginning of class.

Specifically, it looked like a nose then.

Skip figured the kid was lucky he'd gotten caught with a roundhouse kick instead of a karate chop. A knifehand strike from one of Baxter's Deadly Weapons™ might've sheared the nose clean off his face, and then he could have gone as Skeletor for Halloween and maybe he'd at least win a costume contest, because little what-his-nuts definitely wasn't winning any karate contests any time soon. "It only takes three pounds of pressure to break a human nose," was something Skip was very fond of saying, he'd even worked it into his vows when him and Marsha got married, and Skip didn't understand a man who'd cry over a measly three pounds of pressure.

Even an eight-year-old one.

Then the ambulance came and Robert or Mark's dad showed up and beat the shit out of Skip—when you're an eighth-degree black belt, it's not fair to trot out advanced karate techniques against a civilian, even a construction worker who outweighs you by fifty pounds. No, sometimes you've got to take your lumps, and you better believe Skip Baxter didn't *cry* like a little bitch about it.

Granted, he didn't remember *everything* that happened between the moment Robert or Mark's dad shoved a greasy finger in his face and when he woke up in the parking lot with a pair of black eyes and a splitting headache several hours later, but Skip was damn sure he didn't cry.

Given the fortitude he'd shown in the face of adversity, he figured he could be forgiven his failure to lock the fucking door.

Skip pushed the door open and flipped the lights on, hoping nothing had been stolen. Everything looked to be in its proper place, from the white wooden cubbies where students put their shoes to the sea of blue mats extending to the back wall. The glass case full of trophies for tournaments that technically never happened stood intact to one side of the door, and no gang graffiti defaced the Hawk Dragon mural on the wall.

No, everything looked like Skip left it, right down to the unfamiliar man standing in the middle of the room.

Wait, what?

"Mr. Baxter," the man said, crossing his arms—weirdly long appendages, like a chimp or a monkey. He was tall, too, over six feet, and thin, wearing a black silk kimono and Ray-Ban sunglasses. His hair was bleached blonde, gelled and spiked, with the sort of elaborate fade Skip sometimes saw when he taught a charity self-defense class for at-risk youth.

Weirdly, his voice was absurdly high—the kind of sound you'd get if you kicked Alvin, Simon or Theodore in the nuts. That set Skip at ease. Anybody with a voice that high had to be a pussy.

Still, his presence in the dojo was a mystery, and Skip hated mysteries. They made him feel stupid.

"I'm Skip Baxter," Skip said, since nothing else was really coming to him.

The man slowly reached up, pulled his Ray-Bans off, and regarded Skip with one pale blue eye and one black one. "My name, or rather the name bestowed upon me, is Kundarai Saru. Do you know Japanese, Mr. Baxter?"

Skip shrugged. "Domo arigato?"

Saru smiled, revealing very expensive veneers. "I'm afraid that doesn't really apply here, Mr. Baxter.

No, my name means *Glorious Warrior*. A hard-earned name. Many years, many battles. Many enemies vanquished in my quest. A quest that has now brought me to you."

"To me?"

"Tell me, Mr. Baxter, you fancy yourself a *sensei?*"

"Sho nuff," Skip said, getting his composure back. He *was* a sensei, and this was *his* dojo. He hadn't been paying attention to everything this Kundy Ricey Roo fella was saying, in fact most of it went right over his head, but he was Skip Fucking Baxter, the Most Dangerous Man in Turbo City, and even though technically this was an unincorporated area called Agave Gardens, they were only a quarter mile outside the Turbo City city limits, and Skip figured maybe he was the Most Dangerous Man here, too.

Outside of Mark/Robert's dad.

Saru nodded, once. "Very good. And who was your master?"

Skip scoffed. "I'm my own master." He supposed if you wanted to get technical Michael Dudikoff was his master, since he'd watched *American Ninja* about three hundred times (including twice on his wedding night, much to Marsha's chagrin), but he doubted this dipshit with the frosted tips and the lady clothes knew who Michael Dudikoff was.

"Self-taught. Interesting."

"What's this about, anyway? I got a class."

"Your class can wait, Mr. Baxter. I have traveled a long way, across oceans, lakes, rivers, other assorted bodies of water, to be here today. To find my destiny."

"Cool story. What's that got to do with me?"

Saru pointed to the case of trophies. "Every time I

arrive in a new city, I seek out the greatest martial arts masters in town. And I kick. Their. Asses."

Skip flexed his Deadly Weapons™. "I'd love to accommodate you, champ, but I think I'm coming down with something. Cough-cough. So—"

"Prepare to defend yourself!" Saru dropped back into a fighting stance, his hands gracefully arcing through the air.

Skip pulled his phone out. "Like I said, I'm busy, so I'd suggest you beat feet before I call the—"

"Hai-ya!" Saru lashed out with a kick and sent Skip's phone flying. It bounced off the wall, landed on a mat.

"Ow!" Skip said, shaking one of his Deadly Weapons™. He sucked on his thumb, tasted blood. "Not cool, I just got that."

"Worry about me, not your phone." Saru circled, light on his feet like a moth fluttering around the dojo.

Skip backed away towards the door. "Okay, man, I'm out—" *Whumph!*

That sure didn't feel like a door.

Skip slowly turned, found himself face-to-mask with some dude dressed up as a ninja—dark blue pajamas, demon facemask, eyes tight with malice. "Oh shit!"

"*Oh shit* is right, Mr. Baxter. Daisuke?"

The ninja shoved him.

Skip stumbled backwards, spun around, nearly knocked the display case over. His jaw hit the floor—he was surrounded by ninjas. Five, ten, more? They lined the walls, still as statues, some holding bows, katanas, sai.

What do you call a group of ninjas? Skip thought. *A pack? A swarm?*

A fuckload.

"Come, Mr. Baxter!" Saru beckoned to him. "Show me your Hawk Dragon style!"

Skip looked from the ninjas, to Saru, down at his Deadly Weapons™. Asked himself a very important question.

What would Michael Dudikoff do?

Probably *not* piss himself.

Skip Baxter ignored the wet warmth in his crotch and curled his Deadly Weapons™ into fists. They were shaking, undoubtedly from all the chi coursing through his body.

Skip let out the patented Hawk Dragon Martial Arts war cry, a fierce "Ca-caw!" following by a long *fwooooosh* (representing a dragon's fiery breath, of course) and rushed Saru.

He didn't even see the first blow, let alone the last.

NUNCHUCK NICK, SUPER-SERIOUS BUSINESS GUY

NUNCHUCK "NICK" NIKOLOPOULOS struggled against the tightening rope around his neck. Already, he couldn't breathe. He panicked, even though he'd practiced this same position a hundred times—nay, a thousand. It should have been automatic. But now, in a real life-or-death situation, his allegedly well-trained hands simply wouldn't cooperate.

"You . . . shall not . . . best . . . ME!" Nick cried, finally knotting the silk paisley tie into something resembling a Windsor knot. He stepped back, admired his work in the floor-length mirror on the back of his closet door. For a guy who habitually wore a black tank top, white jeans, and leather fingerless gloves, he had to admit he looked pretty okay. Granted, he was wearing one black shoe and one brown shoe, and the tan jacket/red shirt combo wouldn't be causing a stir on the Milan catwalks any time soon, but he'd managed a facsimile of a big-time serious business guy, which was what he was desperately trying to be. In an hour, he'd walk into the biggest meeting of his entire life. Ever since he left Japan, he'd been training for this moment.

Nick picked up the framed picture of his old master, Pierre, from his nightstand and kissed the dour old Frenchman smack on the forehead. Eight thousand miles away, in his mountaintop redoubt in the French Alps, Nick liked to think Pierre sensed the gesture of affection. Granted Pierre probably would have thrown a rock at him if he'd been within rock-throwing distance, but c'est la vie.

"You got this, Nick," he muttered and quickly crossed the bedroom which was also the living room, kitchen, library, self-reflection square, and band rehearsal space and exited his studio apartment into the warm, Turbo City sunshine.

Nick headed down the steps towards a late-model Porsche. And walked past it. He couldn't afford a car, or a cell phone, couldn't even afford rooms, plural, having sunk every last dollar into this new business venture.

Hence the meeting. Hence the importance. Hence the not-fucking-up.

"Morning, Mr. Ortiz!" Nick called to a man he'd never met before, waving animatedly. The man looked confused for a moment, then waved back. Nick didn't make a habit of calling strangers by the wrong name, but he was really in the mood to say hello to someone and he didn't know anybody in Turbo City besides his business partner Rondell. He wanted to share a wave, a smile. Some reassurance everything was going to go smoothly.

Nick left the befuddled man who was probably not

named Ortiz behind and turned left on Corporal Curtis Jackson Boulevard, the main drag cutting across the south end of Turbo City. What his apartment lacked in size, it totally made up for in location and black mold. Which Nick preferred—all those deadly spores kept his immune system working overtime, toughening up his white blood cells.

Jackson Boulevard bustled with energy. People hurried to work, taxis zipped past, fast food restaurants belched out dark, pungent clouds of breakfast exhaust.

All these people, going about their business, Nick thought. *What a strange, beautiful, enticing foreign country.* Business!

The idea that people could make a living by exchanging goods and services rather than brutally murdering clans of rival ninjas blew him away.

Nick waved to a woman in a smart pantsuit, who hurriedly ducked behind a large homeless man wearing a piece of carpet like a poncho. The homeless man jangled a Styrofoam cup with a dollar sign carved into it at Nick, which totally reminded him he'd forgotten to bring change for the bus.

Oh, shit!

Nick sprinted back to his apartment, jumping over an oversized stroller stuffed with triplets and rolling between two dog walkers with approximately three hundred dachshunds between them. He dashed up the stairs, grabbed a handful of change from the jar on the kitchen counter, kissed Pierre's picture once more for good luck, and ran back out onto Jackson Boulevard.

Just in time to see the 8:17 a.m. bus pull away from the curb.

Nick ran after it, dodging traffic, but even he wasn't fast enough to catch a bus. He staggered to a stop in the middle of the street, delivery vans honking at him until he shuffled over to the sidewalk to lean dejectedly against a newspaper kiosk.

"'Scuse me," a scruffy, ball-capped man said.

Nick moved aside so the man could get his paper. Checked his watch—8:19, now. His meeting was scheduled for 9 a.m. sharp at City Hall and he had it on good authority the clerk most definitely did *not* fuck around. If he wanted his business license approved, he was going to have to haul ass.

"The hell's this world coming to," the scruffy man muttered over the sound of rustling newsprint.

"Huh?"

The man shoved a headline Nick's way— MARTIAL ARTS MAVEN MAIMED BY MYSTERIOUS MALEFACTOR. There was a picture of a portly man with his arms bent at weird angles splayed across a mat. The blood-spattered legend HAWK DRAGON MARTIAL ARTS was painted on the wall in the background along with what looked like a really pissed-off chicken.

A flood of memories came rushing back, memories he'd worked hard to forget. "Poor guy," Nick said.

"Not him," the man said, jabbing a finger at the headline. "All this goddamn alliteration! *Martial arts maven's* bad enough, but *maimed by mysterious malefactor?* It's a joke."

The maimed martial arts master on the mat didn't look very funny to Nick.

"I'd better get going," Nick said, "I've got a meeting."

"And *I've* got to write a letter to the editor. Alliteration, my left foot." The man tucked the newspaper under his arm and stalked away, mumbling.

Nick shook his head and broke into a light jog. City Hall was four miles away, but he could make it. He had to.

Otherwise, Fond Dudes was toast.

THE CONVOLUTED ORIGIN STORY OF A DRIVE-THRU FONDUE RESTAURANT

FOND DUDES WAS Rondell's idea.

Mostly.

Rondell was a native son of Turbo City, the product of a typically hardscrabble upbringing. His father worked at a smelting plant, his mother waitressed at a coffee shop. Then they'd traded jobs for a shift to see if anyone would notice, and of course a lot of people did, so they both got fired on the same day. His father got into birdwatching and his mother took up Sudoku, and from there the inevitable drugs, gambling, and shoplifting Hummel figurines from the thrift store. Rondell swore he'd find a way to be his own boss, so no one else could fire him, and he could trade jobs with his (non-existent) wife whenever the fuck he wanted, because he was a goddamn American.

So Rondell scraped, and saved, and pretended to get run over by an old lady in a Cadillac, and pretty soon he'd earned enough to open his own restaurant:

The Crêpes of Wrath, which was kind of like Dick's Last Resort with a French twist. Get yourself a platter of savory galettes and a thorough recounting of your inadequacies delivered by out-of-work standup comedians who expertly zeroed in on every last foible. Turns out people actually *like* being called a piece of shit if the food's good enough. The restaurant was a massive success, and soon it grew to six locations spread out over the entire Turbo City metropolitan area.

Everything was going swimmingly, until the night a beefy, six-foot-tall man in a black tank top and whitewash jeans showed up on the sidewalk outside his Braddockville location with a camping stove and the best goddamn cheese fondue your bitch-ass ever tasted. Before long the mystery man had a line around the block and Rondell's dining room was so empty, the waiters resorted to calling each other fucking asshats.

Amelie, the floor manager, phoned Rondell in a panic. "Mr. Rondell, come quick! This man's taking all our business."

"What do you mean?"

"He's making fondue on the sidewalk. There must be thirty people out there."

"Is he calling them assholes?"

"No, that's the worst part. He's being . . . polite."

Rondell slammed the phone down. "Not on my watch."

Fifteen minutes later, he screeched up in front of the Braddockville location in his '97 Celica, parking in front of a fire hydrant. The guy with the camp stove didn't notice, kept ladling fondue into stolen coffee cups and passing out rounds of French bread. Rondell looked the guy up and down. Big, no doubt, but those were totally gym muscles. A rough and tumble guy like Rondell who came up hard on the infamous east side of Turbo City, with all its smelting plants and coffee shops, would make short work of some protein-powdered douchebag.

"Hey, shithead!" Rondell yelled, marching up to the improvised fondue station. "What do you think you're doing?"

The guy turned and smiled. "Spreading the love, my friend."

"I'm not your fuckin' friend. This is my restaurant, okay? You can't just set up shop on the sidewalk."

The guy frowned. "I can't? Why not?"

"Hey, asshole, there's a line," a woman with a purple afro yelled from down the sidewalk.

Rondell gave her the finger. "For one, this is my spot. And two, you ever heard of the health department?" He pointed angrily at the blue-and-white placard in the restaurant window—a hard-earned C+.

The guy with the camp stove kept smiling. "Look, I don't mean to put you out, and I don't know what the health department's got to do with all this. Here, try some fondue. On the house." He held out a chipped coffee mug with World's Best Boss painted on the side.

"I don't think so."

The woman with the purple afro called, "It's the shit! You don't want, I'll take it!"

Rondell fought the urge to smack the mug away, put the guy in a headlock, make him lap that shit off the sidewalk.

But he didn't.

Despite himself, hands acting independently of his brain, he took the mug and an end-round of French bread.

Dipped, wiped it on the rim of the mug.

CHOMP.

Rondell came to five minutes later, cheese sauce drying on his whiskers. He was out of bread, tongue-fucking the hell out of the mug to get the last little bit of deliciousness inside, panting like he'd just run the Turbo City Marathon.

"That was, was—incredible!"

"Told you," the purple-haired woman said, sipping from her own mug (*Someone's Got a Case of the Mondays*).

"You," he said to the camp stove guy, gently and reverently laying his mug in the orange bucket filled with dirty dishes, "where did you learn to make such great fondue?"

"France, where else?"

Rondell hung around for two more mugs of fondue, both of which he paid for. When business finally dwindled and the guy started breaking down his equipment, Rondell approached him.

"You're one hell of a chef."

"Thank you."

"Would you," and now Rondell looked down at his shoes, toeing a crack in the sidewalk like he was trying to ask Aisha Teller to the eighth-grade dance, "ever want to come work for me?"

The guy squinted at the awning over Crêpes of Wrath. "I dunno. Crêpes and fondue? How's that going to work?"

"They're both French."

"Oh." The guy snapped his camp stove shut. "But what's with all the insults?"

"What do you mean?"

"Food should be fun. It's supposed to make people happy."

Rondell shrugged. "I make people happy. By hurting their feelings. Fucking bitches."

"Well, that's not my style. I appreciate the offer, mister, but I think I'll go my own way." The guy picked up the bucket full of dirties and headed off down the sidewalk.

"Wait!" Rondell called, hurrying to catch up with him. "I've got another idea."

The guy stopped, turning slightly so his profile was visible in moonlight. He had the squarest jaw Rondell had ever seen. "What?"

"We start a new restaurant. Fondue-only. And we won't even make fun of the customers. We'll—" Rondell gulped "—treat them with *dignity*." A half-gallon of fondue threatened to come rocketing back up his throat, but he managed to keep it down.

The guy thought about it for a second, then shrugged. "Okey-dokey. But I get to name it."

"Yeah, sure. Put her there, kid. I'm Rondell."

"Nunchuck Nikolopoulos. My friends call me Nick."

The kid possessed an absolute bone-crusher of a handshake. "Nice to meet you, Nick. So, what do you want to call our little venture?"

Nick looked down at their still-clasped hands. "Fond Dudes. Because there's nothing more important than cheese and friendship!" He wrapped

Rondell up in a hug at least twice as tight as his handshake. "The logo's going to be a silhouette of us hugging!"

"Urk . . . good . . . idea."

They quickly worked out the details. Rondell leased a former Gutbuster off Jackson Boulevard, which was nice because they had a drive-thru and, in the proper receptacle, fondue could be enjoyed on the go. Nick loved the idea—fondue for the people, he raved. The idea of taking a snooty French dish and democratizing it really appealed to him.

Rondell just figured people would buy the shit. Hell, they ate the pseudo-cheese sauce from 7-11. They'd go bananas for real fondue at fast food prices.

Unfortunately, two weeks before the big opening, the doucheclown health inspector downgraded that C+ on his Braddockville location, threatening to shut Rondell down completely if he kept letting the chefs spit in the food (with a $12.99 upcharge, of course). Rondell didn't want to screw up the deal and lose the cash he'd already invested, so he hit on a compromise.

Put Nick, and only Nick, on the business license.

Ordinarily, he'd never take a risk like that, but this was Nick. The guy was utterly guileless, a big goofy kid in an action hero's body.

What could possibly go wrong?

THE GANGS OF TURBO CITY

THIRTEEN MINUTES TO GO. Nick pumped his arms and legs furiously, darting around pedestrians. The curling spire of City Hall stuck out from behind the Gruber Building, beckoning him.

So close.

And yet so far. Farther than a thirteen-minute run, at least. A giant robot could carry him there in seconds, if one was nearby and/or existed, but no. He was screwed.

Unless . . .

He cut through Kersey Park.

The park, a rare splash of green amongst the glass and steel towers of downtown Turbo City, lay between him and City Hall. The smart move was to take the long way around. That's what any self-respecting Turbosian would do. Nick hadn't lived in the city very long, but the one mantra he'd heard repeated again and again, from short order cooks at greasy spoons to friendly mailpeople, was this:

Stay the hell away from Kersey Park. Especially during the day.

19

At night, sure, take your chances. Ever since the mayor implemented a 9pm curfew for criminals, the park was relatively safe after dark. But during the day?

Kersey Park made the most war-torn Syrian village look like a fucking Build-A-Bear workshop.

Nick paused at the entrance of the park, jogging in place. If he sprinted through the park, he'd be at City Hall in under five minutes. Unless he got into a scuffle with any local hooligans, which might tack another fifteen or sixteen seconds onto his trip, but he'd still make it.

The only problem was, if he ran into trouble, he couldn't fight back. Ever since the thing with his old master— the ninjutsu one, not the fondue one—he'd taken a vow of pacifism. Never again would he raise a hand or elbow or knee in anger.

Nick chanced a glance at his watch—8:53.

No choice.

Nick dashed into the park, down an idyllic, winding trail. Tecate Cypress and Palo Blanco rose thick and high on either side of the path. He rounded a bend, saw no one, kept going, constantly aware of the ticking second hand on his watch. Through every break in the trees above, he sought out signs of his destination, assurances he was on the right path.

The Gruber Building bowed out of view, City Hall neared.

Close, so close.

8:56.

The end of the trail lay ahead. Nick turned on the afterburners, picturing some smiling clerk stamping his paperwork, using her municipal magic to abracadabra him from an itinerant ex-ninja fondue chef into a real live business owner. A respectable pillar of the community. The kind of man who—

Willowy branches shook overhead. Dark shapes fell from the trees in front of him, behind him, oversized acorns landing with a soft *tumph,* kicking up clouds of dust.

Voices laughed, the sort of jolly, deep-throated ho-ho-ho one might hear at a well-heeled country club.

Nick came to a stop, reflexively dropped back into a fighting stance.

The shapes closed in, resolving themselves into a gang of youths. All were dandy-clad, the leader a monocled specimen leaning on a cane topped with a finely-carved ivory lion and blocking the park exit. The rest, in sharkskin and cashmere, double-breasted and three-pieces, circled.

Brandishing chains, baseball bats, knives.

"Ahem!" the leader cried. "Let this meeting of the Kerseyshire Hunting Club come to order!"

"Indubitably," the others responded.

Nick pivoted slowly. They'd done a fine job of surrounding him, he really was out of practice.

8:57.

"What do you want?" Nick asked. "I need to get to City Hall."

Monocle Man smirked. "A politician, you say?"

"No. A simple businessman."

"Mm. What, pray tell, is your business?"

"Sucking dick, probably!" cried a ruffian in a Sherlock Holmes hat.

"Cyril, how many times do I have to tell you? *Language.*"

Cyril bowed his head, face reddening.

"Look," Nick said, "I'm just trying to go like twenty feet that way. You guys think you could let me on my way?"

"I'm afraid that's impossible, chap. Not without a tribute."

"Tribute?"

Monocle Man swept a hand across the trail, indicating the slavering band of hooligans. "Do you think such finery grows on trees? Ha! Ha-ha!"

The others joined in, laughing wildly, throwing arms about their fellows.

"Ha?" Nick said. He hated feeling left out.

"No!" Monocle Man cried, stamping the ground with his cane. "We collect tribute from well-dressed gentlemen like yourself, and thus maintain our impeccable appearance. Oh, why in the world am I *explaining* this, when we could sing you our song? Horace?"

A slide-whistle blew somewhere over to Nick's six.

"And a-one, and a-two—"

"*Oh, we are the Kerseyshire Hunting Club, Sons of Kersey are we—*"

Nick glanced down at his watch—8:58.

"*You'll know us by our Houndstooth jackets, argyle socks aplenty—*"

On the one hand, he'd taken a vow.

On the other hand, that vow was starting to seem *really* inconvenient.

Nick tensed imperceptibly, a tightly-wound spring, and then—

SHIT POPPED THE FUCK OFF.

Nick spun, throwing the full force of his body into

a roundhouse kick that shattered the slide-whistle man's jaw. Momentum carried him into a handspring off the ground, his mismatched shoes crashed into another tough's chest, smashing his collarbone to bits. Nick landed on his feet, jumped into the air and grabbed a branch.

Which snapped off in his hands. Nick plummeted towards the ground, tucked and rolled, came up and beaned Sherlock in the skull. The tough crumpled to the ground.

Nobody was singing any more.

A few of them cried *oh dear* and ran off into the woods, leaving Nick alone with Monocle Man.

Monocle Man looked at the twitching bodies of his friends, the fleeing forms of guys who used to be his friends. Back at Nick. "Um—"

Nick snatched the cane out of his hands and pushed him, hard. Monocle Man fell on his ass, the monocle popping out to dangle from its gold chain.

"Please," Monocle Man said. "I've got monogrammed handkerchiefs, cufflinks—"

"Like I said, I'm only trying to get to City Hall. Although," Nick hefted the cane, "I guess this completes my ensemble."

8:59.

Nick took off, leaving the dandy highwayman to contemplate the loss of both cane and reputation. He left the park, bounded up the steps of City Hall, surrendered the cane to a security card who insisted it looked like a weapon, and found himself in line at the city clerk's window at 9 a.m. sharp.

A little sweaty, but on time.

Just like a real fucking business guy.

The opaque glass window slid to the side. A purple fingernail motioned Nick forward.

"Hello," Nick said, lowering his voice to sound more professional. "I'm Ni—uh, MISTER Nikolopoulos. Here for my 9 a.m."

The city clerk click-clacked on her keyboard a few times. "Says here you're my 9:15."

"Oh," Nick said.

"Mr. Ortiz is at 9. Mr. Ortiz? Is there a Mr. Ortiz here?"

A guy with a handlebar mustache raised his hand. He was definitely not the same Mr. Ortiz Nick said good morning to almost an hour before, who probably wasn't named Mr. Ortiz at all.

Nick backed away from the window and took a seat in a plastic chair. Not comfortable, but he'd grown up sleeping on a literal bed of nails, and the discomfort kept him from thinking about the fact he'd had plenty of time to cut around the park, didn't have to violate his oath after all.

He looked around the room until he found the perfect distraction. A silent TV above the wall recounted the morning's news. The story about the dojo beating was getting top billing. Nick squinted at the chevron below the lip-syncing anchors— BREAKING, SECOND MARTIAL ARTIST ATTACKED IN ARMSTRONG CORNERS.

That's just north of here, Nick thought. *Huh.*

All the talk about martial arts reminded him of things he'd rather forget, so he pulled out his application. He double-checked his name. The name of the business. The address. Made sure he hadn't accidentally written anything in the angry yellow block marked RESERVED FOR CITY CLERK'S USE ONLY. He had not.

"Mr. Niko—nik—snuffalupagus?" the clerk called.

"That's me," Nick said brightly, rising from the chair and handing his application to the clerk.

Her eyes went wide. "Your name's . . . Nunchuck?"

Nick nodded.

"Kind of a weird name, don't you think?"

"I don't know, you've met a Chuck before, right?"

"My sister's husband," the clerk said.

"Now you've met a Nunchuck. I go by Nick."

"Mmmhmm," she said, and continued scanning. She held the application one-handed so the other could tap her long, sparkly purple nails on the desk to the tune of Naughty by Nature's "O.P.P.," a song Nick wouldn't recognize as he'd spent much of the early '90s learning geometry and assassinating minor Yakuza figures. Even though he didn't know the song, Nick started tapping his own foot in time, until he realized that probably didn't look very professional.

"Hmmhmmm," the clerk said again. She stopped tapping.

Nick's heart skipped a beat—something was wrong! But then she started up again, C+C Music Factory, and Nick actually knew that one because it'd been all the rage in Japan. He'd even danced to it at the Inter-Dojo Ninja Sock Hop, with Kanna—

Nick's pleasant expression fell apart. He cleared his mind and forced another smile.

"Wait here." The clerk slid off her stool.

"Is something wro—" Nick asked, but she'd already disappeared into the back.

Seconds crept by. Nick wondered what he could

have screwed up. Being named *Nunchuck,* maybe, but that wasn't his fault. People didn't get to pick their own names, that would be ridiculous.

"Okay," the clerk said, returning to the window. "Made some copies." She shoved a sheaf of papers at Nick. "Looks like everything's in order."

Nick beamed. "You mean—"

"All you have to do is get the mayor's signature, and you're in business."

"How do I do that?"

The clerk pointed at the ceiling. "Third floor. Tell his secretary you need a business license. Might have to wait—"

"Thank you!" Nick cried, clutching the papers to his chest. Everything was coming together. Before he knew it, he'd be doling out the best darn fondue in Turbo—

The pressure in the room dropped. Nick's heartbeat slowed to a crawl. All the little hairs on his neck stood at attention.

"Mrs. Wang?" the clerk called. "There a Mrs. Wang here?"

And then Nick heard it, muffled by two floors of insulation and steel beams and a lethal amount of asbestos.

BAM!

POW!

An untrained listener might have chalked the noises up to a couple of freewheeling furniture movers, but no amount of vows could deafen Nick's highly-trained ninja ears.

"Something's wrong," Nick said.

"Sure is," the clerk said. "Mrs. Wang's not due for another three hours. Damn computer."

"Not that," Nick said, stuffing his application in his pocket and hurrying for the stairwell. He pushed through the door. Now he could hear everything.

Screaming. Lots and lots of fucking screaming.

Nick paused, one hand on the railing. He'd already violated his vow of pacifism once that morning. If he were to violate it again, what kind of a vow would it even be?

A loud banging echoed in the stairwell, maybe a file cabinet tipping over. "Help!" someone shrieked, their shrill voice cutting through two floors of municipal bureaucracy.

Nick bit his lip. Before the pacifism vow, he'd taken others, more vows than most people took in their entire lifetime. He did the math, adding up the different promises he'd made to himself, his various masters, the world, and most importantly the mighty Fox God, Mr. Shifty Whiskers, Ph.D.

Something terrible was happening, and he couldn't just stand by listening to people screaming and office furniture being treated roughly.

And if something happened to the mayor who would sign his business license?

Quickly, Nick undid the semi-Windsor knot at his neck and wrapped the tie around his head. Then he ran up the stairs, two at a time, rushing towards the commotion.

And motherfucking destiny.

DIZZONER

MAYOR JOE DIFORMAGGIO huddled behind his desk, dripping sweat onto the blue silk sash across his chest that read *Ms. Turbo City 2014*. He didn't know what was going on, but there were a lot of loud and scary noises, and he was still pretty preoccupied by the fact that the dry cleaners had given him the wrong sash. He blamed his valet, Chuck. The guy was an idiot, muttered "Green means go!" or "Red means stop" at every light. Unless it was yellow, in which case he screamed, took his foot off the pedal, and drifted through the intersection with his hands clamped firmly over his eyes. Mayor Joe might've fired Chuck, but he was married to the city clerk's sister, and he was not about to fuck with Rhonda, not for love or money or even a driver with the mental capacity of a salt-sprinkled slug.

"I need a sit-rep!" Stone Ironside, his chief of security, yelled into a crackling walkie-talkie. No sit-rep came back, just a bunch of anguished wails and heavy thumps.

Mayor Joe peeked out from behind the desk. "Anything?"

Stone shook his head stoically. He crouched to one

28

side of the doorframe, a .45 semi-automatic held tightly in his left hand.

"Ozarks!" Mayor Joe hissed. Most guys would have said *rats* or *that's some bullshit* in a situation like this, but not Mayor Joe. Nothing pissed him off more than geology.

"Bzzzt!" screeched the walkie-talkie. "Killing us . . . dear G—"

"That doesn't sound good."

"No sir, it does not," Stone said. "I've radioed for backup, but—"

WHAM! Something crashed into the door from the other side, sending Stone stumbling back. He braced himself against the desk, an imposing oak affair six good men gave their lives to move up to the third floor, aimed his gun at the door.

"I don't suppose you know how to use one of these," he said.

Mayor Joe shook his head.

BRAM! The door juddered in its frame.

"Gah!" Mayor Joe screamed, crouching down even lower, trying to make himself as small as a city councilman, or at least the deputy mayor. It didn't work, because the deputy mayor was a 1/4 scale statue of Mayor Joe himself, with a thick mustache painted above his upper lip so no one would get wise. Most of the Turbo City higher-ups were the same, statues or mannequins or dogs in funny hats. Needed to keep the budget balanced somehow, and because Mayor Joe had a bitchin' case of insomnia he was able to do most of the big-ticket jobs without anyone noticing. Well, also because the *real work* was done by people like Rhonda, but the insomnia didn't hurt. He spent his nights scheduling emails to go out at various times the following day from dozens of different fictional bureaucrats.

"What're we going to do?" Mayor Joe asked.

Stone looked around, perhaps searching for a friendly unit of Navy Seals or British SAS he'd missed up until now. "We block the door. Come on, help me with your desk."

"Help . . . you?" A lifelong politician, the concept of *helping* people was as foreign to Mayor Joe as advanced calculus to a Lhasa Apso. Or to Mayor Joe.

Stone leaned into one corner of the desk, the corded muscles in his neck popping. "Get the other end."

Mayor Joe went to the side of the desk opposite Stone and pushed with all his might, which is to say barely at all.

"The *other* other end," Stone said. "You're—"

CRASH!

The wood around the doorknob splintered. Whoever was banging on his door was doing a much better job of it than Mayor Joe's bodyguard was barricading the thing.

"Mayor! Come on."

Hurrying to the other side of the desk, Mayor Joe took up a position next to Stone, trying his best to mimic the other man's posture.

"On three," Stone said. "One, two—"

A fist burst through the door, the doorknob fell to the ground with a clunk.

Stone pulled his gun and fired four quick shots through the door.

The fist disappeared. Mayor Joe clamped his

hands down hard over his earsies, scowling at the bodyguard. "Too loud," he shouted, but he couldn't even hear himself so he doubted the message got through to Stone. He made a mental note to fire him when all this was over—destroying his mayoral ear drums ran contrary to the head of security's prime directive to protect him at all costs.

Stone yanked at his sleeve, motioned to the desk. Mayor Joe reluctantly removed his hands from his still-ringing ears and placed them against the heavy mahogany.

"Now," Stone said.

Mayor Joe pushed. Pushed with all his might. His arms and legs screamed with the exertion, sweat broke out on his brow. His *teeth* hurt. He closed his eyes, pictured himself cutting the ribbon at his long-planned but so far non-existent Museum of Mayoral Achievement with a gigantic pair of novelty scissors, wondered where he might actually find a gigantic pair of novelty scissors, like they have to make those things, right? You see them in movies, TV. Maybe it was like a *Field of Dreams* thing. If he built the museum, somebody would show up to the opening ceremony with oversized scissors for him. Or, better yet, maybe if he found a big enough pair of scissors the museum would build itself.

He'd just begun fantasizing about what sorts of goodies one might find in the gift shop (t-shirts with his face? Life-size replicas of the deputy mayor? Sashes reading "Mayor—JK?" the possibilities were literally endless) when the desk thunked against the battered door frame.

"We did it!" Mayor Joe cried, raising his hands

high in celebration. This was the first time he'd actually accomplished something since taking office fifteen years before. "That was incredible. I think I'm going to try doing things more often."

"What?"

Mayor Joe smiled, turning away from the superbly-barricaded door he'd helped with—nay, masterminded. A brilliant idea, really, one sure to change the fortunes of Turbo City for the better, to uplift even the most wretched—

Footsteps pattered across the fourth floor above their heads.

Stone pointed his gun at the ceiling, trying to track the noise. "Bastards. Come on, come on—"

The footsteps stopped.

"Gotcha now," Stone said, finger brushing the trigger.

"No!" Mayor Joe shouted, diving forward and knocking the gun out of Stone's hand. The .45 skidded across the room and came to rest underneath a shelf of never-read books the mayor's publicist picked out.

"What the hell?" Stone snarled, grabbing Mayor Joe by his sash.

The mayor cowered. "My ears."

"What?"

"The gun hurts my ears," Mayor Joe said, pointing a shaking finger at one ear, then the other, in case Stone didn't get it. He wasn't the sharpest knife in the drawer.

"The gun hurts your ears? My gun is here to protect you. God damn it." Stone pushed the mayor away.

Mayor Joe hurriedly straightened his askew

sash—even if it did say *Ms. Turbo City 2014,* he didn't want to look sloppy for the news cameras, who'd surely be arriving any minute.

Stone grabbed his gun off the floor and took up a position by the window, the morning sun silhouetting him in a very dramatic fashion. "Let's get one thing straight, buster. I'm trying to get us both out of here, alive. So until then, I'm the fucking mayor, capisce? You do exactly what I say, when I say it."

Mayor Joe frowned, pointing to his sash. "But I'm the mayor."

Stone groaned. "It's a figure of speech. Now, we have to—"

Shadows flashed in the window behind Stone.

Then it exploded.

CITY HALL? MORE LIKE SHITTY HALL AMIRITE?

THE HALLWAY LOOKED like a fucking warzone.

Smashed furniture, scarred walls, liberal amounts of blood splashed over every possible surface. Moans and wails from unseen victims echoed off the tile. The scent of death hung thick in the air. Nick felt sick—he'd traveled thousands of miles to get away from that scent, and now it had found him again.

The whole situation baffled him—who'd attack City Hall like this?

Terrorists, maybe. Or thieves pretending to be terrorists so they could steal hundreds of millions of dollars in untraceable bearer bonds.

Somebody had to stop them.

Nick crept down the hallway. He peeked into the first office—a man, maybe a few years younger than Nick himself, lay slumped over his desk, a thick crimson stain spreading out from beneath his once-white shirt.

Disturbing, but the thing that really got Nick's attention was the katana sticking out of his back.

When did terrorists start using katana? Guns, box cutters, rental trucks filled with weaponized fertilizer, sure, but katana? That was some ninja shit.

Wind tickled his ears. Nick ducked, two ninja stars zipping over his head and embedding themselves in the drywall above the poor, katana-skewered dead man who was probably an accountant or something, and spun around.

A ninja stood in the hallway, clad head-to-toe in a black shinobi shōzoku, a pair of lightly-curved kama in his hands.

Nick shuddered at the sight—beating up a gang of well-dressed dandies in the park was one thing, but ninja? He hadn't been in a real fight in years, or even trained. Facing off against an actual-factual ninja now was like showing up to the 100-meter dash after spending a decade eating nachos and watching *Shark Tank*.

The ninja charged.

Nick jumped back, landing on the desk next to the dead guy, and yanked the katana out of his back with a wet *spluch*. Blood splattered him, ruining his serious business guy clothes, and Nick fervently hoped the mayor wouldn't hold that against him whenever he eventually made it to the end of the hallway and asked him to sign his business license.

The ninja leapt into the air, kama poised to rip him apart. Nick swung the katana, but the ninja twisted away at the last second and landed behind the desk.

Nick used the opportunity to dive out into the hallway, rolling and slamming into the opposite wall. He held onto the katana, took a few steps down the hallway and turned.

"Hai!" the ninja screamed, dashing out of the office and slashing at the air with the *kama*, the blades moving faster than an industrial thresher.

Nick swung the katana, sparks glancing off the ninja's curved blades. He batted them away, dropped to a squat and slashed at the ninja's knees, but his assailant somersaulted over him. Pain blossomed in Nick's shoulder—a long red slash had ripped apart both suit jacket and flesh. Blood ran freely, soaking his dress shirt.

Nick barely got the katana up in time to block the next volley of blows. The ninja kept screaming at him, *hai* this and *hai-ya* that, which was totally rude because if he'd taken like a minute to talk maybe they could have sorted this whole thing out, discovered they both really liked knock-knock jokes or cookie dough ice cream or jacking off in the rain, but no, the ninja was intent on goring Nick, which made Nick wonder if maybe he'd met the guy before, if the guy had some sort of beef with him, but said guy was wearing a shinobi shōzoku and aside from the really flamboyant dudes who'd glue a bunch of rhinestones to the back of their jacket in the shape of a dragon or something, it was practically impossible to tell ninja apart.

Nick blocked a few more blows, but the ninja pressed his advantage, backing Nick down the hallway. Nick hazarded a front kick, the ninja jumped back and swiped with the kama, taking a chunk out of Nick's leg.

"Shit!" Another flesh wound, but he couldn't afford to lose much more blood, he needed that shit.

The ninja lunged, kama raised high. Nick turned

sideways. The kama swished through the air and narrowly missed him, crashing against the tile floor. Nick threw a flying knee and nailed the ninja in his stupid masked face. The ninja's head snapped back, one kama went flying end-over-end down the hallway and embedded itself in an office door.

Nick swept downwards with the katana, angling to take the ninja's fucking head off. The ninja monkey-crawled away, the katana lodged in an up-ended bookcase with a light shunk.

Before Nick could yank the katana out, the ninja lunged at him again with his remaining kama. Nick abandoned the sword and jumped back a few feet into a puddle of something gross and wet that totally used to be inside someone's body until fairly recently. He slipped, landing heavily on his back, air knocked out of him.

The ninja loomed over him, kama held high. Dark splotches along the blade's teeth indicated it had been well-used.

And was about to be well-used again.

Nick threw his legs up, trying to keep the blade away from his soft, squishy bits—

Something whistled through the air, a black manrikigusari chain wrapped around the ninja's throat. He dropped the kama, hands struggling against the chain. Whoever was on the other end gave it the briefest of tugs and snapped his neck with a loud CRACK. The ninja swayed and tumbled, landing heavily on top of Nick.

Nick shoved the dead ninja off, jumping to his feet. Perhaps the Arthashastra said "the enemy of my enemy is my friend," but in Nick's experience the enemy of your enemy could immediately transmogrify into also *your* enemy the second the other guy was dead.

Another ninja waited at the end of the hallway, holding the manriki chain two-fisted. This ninja was clad in powder-blue, and from the way the shinobi shōzoku hugged the curves of her body it was clearly a lady-ninja. Nick had grown up with plenty of lady-ninjas, knew they were just as deadly as dude-ninjas (situationally moreso—men will relax in the company of strange women). The katana was a good five feet away, but Nick doubted he'd make it.

So, he tried something totally different.

He raised his hands, plastered his trademark easygoing smile on his face, and said, "Hey there."

The lady-ninja stared at him for the longest second of his life.

Then she yanked her mask off. She shook out her long, glossy black hair and looked Nick in the eye.

"Nick," Kanna said, a slight smile playing across her face. "What the fuck are you doing here?"

Nick's mouth went dry. He tried to think of something suave or profound to say, but he couldn't. Kanna. After all this time. "I'm opening a drive-thru fondue restaurant."

"God, you're a weirdo. It's good to see you, Nick."

"It is?" The last time they'd seen each other, a decade before, he accidentally killed the shit out of her father and fled Clan Hanasu Nezumi in disgrace.

"Well, yeah—" Kanna whirled, snapping the *manriki* down the hallway and wrapping it around the ankle of a silently-charging ninja. She yanked, snapping his ankle in one smooth motion.

"Arggh!" the ninja screamed.

Kanna tugged her chain again. The ninja flew down the hallway, skidded to a stop at her feet. She pulled a tantō from her tunic and swiftly dispatched him, stabbing the short sword through his neck. The ninja gurgled a few times, and then fell silent.

"What are you doing here, Kanna?" Nick asked.

Kanna leaned down and wiped the tantō clean on the dead ninja's shinobi shōzoku. "No time. Come on, the mayor's in danger." She slipped the tantō back into her tunic and took off down the hallway.

Nick grabbed the katana and ran to catch up with her.

"Katana, eh?" Kanna said, casting him a sidelong glance. "You were never much of an edged-weapon guy. You were always so much better with—"

"Let's go find the mayor," Nick muttered. "I've got a business license that needs signing."

They slowed at a bend in the hallway. Nick listened for muffled breathing, or incredibly-slow ninja heartbeats, or the rustle of badass black trousers.

Nothing.

"Clear," he mouthed.

Kanna nodded and disappeared around the corner.

Nick followed, adjusting his grip on the katana. The next hallway looked much like the previous one, both in its construction and layout as well as being strewn with severed body parts and covered in drying gouts of bodily fluids. Most of the dead bodies here wore suits. One decapitated head still had an earpiece in, and the odd severed hand still wrapped around the butt of a semi-automatic pistol.

The door at the end of the hall featured a massive gold sign that read *Hizzoner Joseph J. DiFormaggio, Mayor of Turbo City*. A smaller sign underneath said the same thing. And one even smaller sign repeated the message, except there wasn't enough room for the "Of Turbo City" part, or the mayor's redundant middle initial.

"What kind of a mayor needs three signs on his door?" Kanna asked.

"I don't know," Nick said. He'd never owned a door with his name on it before, let alone one with his name in triplicate. Gave him an idea, actually. He whipped out the notepad from his back pocket and quickly wrote it down.

"What are you doing?"

Nick held up the notepad. "Little trick I picked up. If you get an idea, write it down. So you won't forget." He tapped the side of his forehead.

"Nick, everyone does that."

"They do?"

"Yep." Kanna pulled a notebook from her tunic. "See?"

Nick leaned forward, squinting at the page.

Kanna's To-Do List:
~~Kill asshole ninjas~~
~~Kill more asshole ninjas~~
Save the stupid jerk mayor
Finish My Heart is a Chainsaw

"*My Heart is a Chainsaw* was pretty good," Nick said. "I liked that part when—"

Kanna clamped a hand over his mouth. "It says *finish,* not *reread,* jackass."

Nick offered a muffled "Sorry."

"It's okay. Slasher novels come after saving the stupid jerk mayor, so . . ."

They took up positions on either side of the hallway, peeking in the doors in case another asshole ninja was getting ready to leap out at them. None did. Except for the dead bodyguards, the hallway appeared completely empty.

Nick pressed his ear to the mayor's door. Inside, someone was struggling to breathe.

"Come on," he said, reaching for the doorknob. There wasn't one.

"Wait." Kanna grabbed his forearm. "What if it's a trap?"

"Could be," Nick said, electricity shooting up and down his arm from her touch. "What else can we do?"

Kanna bit her lip. "Okay. Boot the door, I'll go low, you go high."

Nick reared back and kicked the door hard as he could.

It didn't budge.

"Huh," Nick said. Usually when he kicked something, it broke, or exploded, or at least said *ow, stop it*.

Kanna peered through the hole in the door where the doorknob was supposed to be. "There's a big desk blocking the door."

"Want me to kick it again?"

"Can't hurt."

Nick kicked the door again, and again, and again, the impact shooting painfully up his legs. Other than a few scuff marks, nothing happened.

"You're a little out of shape, huh?"

"No." Nick backed up, got a running start, launched himself into the air. His foot slammed into the door, punching a hole through the wood six inches above the doorknob. He landed awkwardly, but the door had a brand-new hole in it, so that was dope.

"Loop your manriki through," Nick said. "We'll pull this door off its hinges."

"Stupid door," Kanna said, easing the chain through one hole and out the other. She handed one end to Nick.

Nick gripped the chain. "On three?"

"On three. *Ichi, ni—*"

"San!" they yelled in unison, each jerking the chain as hard as they could.

Hinges creaked with promise.

"Again," Kanna said. More yanking, more creaking.

"Third time's usually the charm," Nick said. They pulled again, the hinges kept screaming but the door held fast.

"Too obvious," Kanna said. "Fourth time's the real charm."

"That's not even a—"

"Pull!"

Grrrrrrrrrrrrrrrrrrrrrrrrrnnnnnnnnnnnn!

The door came loose, careening towards the floor. Nick barely got out of the way. He grabbed the katana again and followed Kanna through the now-open doorway.

42

A badly-wounded man lay on the floor beneath a shattered window, covered in blood and broken glass. He held a hand over a gash on his neck, but from the amount of blood already soaked into the carpet Nick knew trying to staunch the flow was pointless.

The man moaned softly. "I couldn't stop them. They, they took him."

"Who did?" Nick asked.

"Kundarai Saru," Kanna said.

A chill ran down Nick's spine. "Saru is here? In Turbo City?"

"I've been tracking the bastard. Almost caught him in Melbourne, came close again in Vienna. Now I'm here." She turned to Nick. "And so are you."

"Gah—" the man on the floor said, then his hand fell away from his neck and he lay still.

Outside, sirens wailed.

"We need to go," Kanna said. "Ninjas all look the same to the cops."

Nick nodded, staring out the window, wondering where they'd taken the mayor and who the heck was going to sign his business license.

KURGAN'S LAW

NICK AND KANNA ducked into an alley, narrowly avoiding a speeding police car. They hunkered down behind a dumpster. A whole column of cop cars and SWAT vans sped past. The dumpster smelled like moldy cheese. Nick figured he probably didn't smell much better, since his clothes were covered in blood and bile and he'd severely underestimated how much running and fighting getting a business license entailed. He tried to give himself a surreptitious sniff, only to catch a whiff of Kanna instead.

She still smelled like jasmine, orange blossoms, and ham-and-cheese Hot Pockets.

Nick shivered and leaned away from her. "What are we going to do?"

"I've got a safehouse, not far from here."

"Me too. We could go to mine."

Kanna arched an eyebrow. "Does your safehouse have more than one pair of underwear on the floor?"

"Okay, let's go to yours."

"This way." Kanna headed off down the alley.

Nick followed, pulling off his jacket. He immediately felt better. Every sleeve was a straitjacket waiting to happen, and he was going to need all the arm freedom he could get. Plus, the jacket was really gross. He wondered if every visitor to City Hall ended up doused with bodily fluids, or if he was especially lucky.

At the end of the alley, Kanna jumped up and grabbed the hanging ladder of a fire escape and motioned for Nick to do the same. Nick easily caught the handle and pulled himself up. The fire escape swayed slightly under their combined weight, creaking with every rung either of them ascended, but held.

The fire escape ended a few feet south of the roof. Kanna braced herself and did a backflip off the ladder, disappearing over the lip. Nick readied himself to jump, but he hadn't done much backflipping in years. Front flips, sure, that was 90% of basic training for a fondue apprentice, but just because you can flip forward doesn't mean you can flip backwards, and vice versa. Millions of people across the world take such things for granted and die horribly as a result.

"Little help?" Nick called.

"Seriously?" Kanna said, but snaked her manriki down over the side anyway.

A cop car turned down the alley, blaring.

He grabbed the manriki, Kanna pulled him up to the roof, and if the passing cops saw anything at all it was only a pair of mismatched dress shoes disappearing over the ledge. The car didn't even slow down.

They ran across the roof, leapt in unison to the next building. For a moment Nick found himself back in Mie Prefecture, vaulting across bamboo-thatched rooftops while cherry blossoms fell lazily all around him, he and Kanna leap-frogging each other, pushing one another to be faster, better. To honor their master, and their spiritual ancestors, the thousands of faceless shinobi who'd come before them, all the way back to the founder of Clan Hanasu Nezumi, the fabled Orenji-iro no Kame himself, who crafted the legendary Sticks of Heaven from a lightning-blasted Ōku tree and a chain forged from the melted-down katanas of the one hundred Tsumasaki warriors he'd bested in battle. With the Sticks of Heaven, Orenji-iro no Kame cut a bloody swath across Japan, annihilating anyone who dared oppose him. And yet, despite his martial prowess and ruthlessness, Orenji-iro was no mere tyrant. It was said he only emerged from his redoubt far beneath the cobblestone streets of Kyoto to right wrongs, hunt bandits, and depose warlords who conducted themselves without honor, who ignored the precepts of Bushido for personal gain.

Like the Tsumasaki, his sworn enemies. Ever since the murder of his equally legendary master, Misutāmausu, and his brothers Ao, Murasakino, and Aka at the hands of the Tsumasaki clan leader, the dreaded Shogun Togatta Otoko, Orenji-iro hunted them day and night. The stories said it took a hundred years, but Orenji-iro finally cornered Togatta Otoko, breaking every bone in his body with the Sticks of Heaven and leaving him to live out his days as an invalid, lying in the dark on a straw pallet, sipping soup brought to him by the old women of the village who also peed in it because fuck that guy.

Nick and Kanna jumped to the next rooftop, displacing a flock of pigeons.

SCREEEECH!

A horrible staticky sound rent the sky. Nick thought maybe there were some more pigeons, with razor blades tied to their feet like champion cockfighters, swooping down to cut him to ribbons, but it was just a big-ass blimp—the pigeons of the aeronautical world.

"I hate blimps," Nick growled.

"Wait," Kanna said, pausing on the edge of the roof. "Is that—"

A gigantic TV screen on the side of the blimp lit up, showing an extreme closeup of a man's nose hairs.

"No, I said pan out!" an array of loudspeakers mounted under the blimp screamed.

Nick and Kanna exchanged an uneasy glance.

The camera backed away, revealing a guy with a very angular face, an outdated soul patch and shockingly blonde hair. Like a skinnier Guy Fieri.

That really pissed Nick off.

"Kundarai Saru!" Nick exclaimed. He'd never much liked Saru, and now here he was, on the side of a blimp.

"You can swing a ninjato but you can't point a fucking camera in the right direction? Jesus, Daisuke."

"Sorry," someone said offscreen, presumably Daisuke, although Nick couldn't be sure since there weren't any closed captions. Extremely inconsiderate to any deaf Turbosians who might be watching.

"Turbo City!" Saru shouted into the camera. "My name is Kundarai Saru."

"Duh," Kanna said. "Stupid jerk."

"I have traveled far in search of my destiny. And now, I have found it. Daisuke?"

The camera pulled back, revealing Saru standing next to a very frightened Mayor Joe. Hizzoner was duct taped to a chair and gagged, blinking furiously at the camera.

"As you can see, I have kidnapped your mayor."

"No shit," Kanna muttered.

"You're probably wondering why I would do such a thing. The answer is simple. I am going to kick. His. Ass!"

The mayor shook his head furiously, eyes wide.

"I don't get it," Kanna said. "Why didn't he beat the shit out of him at City Hall?"

"You moronic Turbosians," Saru continued, "and your antiquated laws. Since none of you can read, I'll explain. Slowly." Saru unfurled a long vellum scroll, filled with intricate handwriting, and jabbed a finger at the legend at the top.

Laws and By-Laws of Spring Bay, USA

"Spring Bay?" Kanna asked. "But—"

"It's like *Truth or Consequences*," Nick explained. "The town in New Mexico? Changed their name to suck up to some game show. Spring Bay did the same thing back in the '90s. They were super broke and thought they could get NEC to bail them out if they renamed themselves after the TurboGrafx-16."

"The what now?"

"It was a video game console."

Kanna nodded. "Ohh, like Sega CD."

"Except not as successful."

Saru shook the scroll at the camera. "May I direct

your collective attention to Section 4B, Paragraph Q. Specifically," he leered at the camera, "Kurgan's Law."

"I'm really struggling to keep up with this shit," Kanna said.

"Back in '86, everybody saw *Highlander* and got really excited, there was this ballot initiative—"

"Kurgan's Law," Saru said, "clearly states that *whosoever beats the ever-loving shit out of the mayor*—that's a direct quote—*becomes him.* Of course, there's a bunch of provisions in here, fight must be one-on-one, foreign objects are *strictly* forbidden, in case of loss the former mayor is still covered under the city's dental plan in perpetuity, et cetera et cetera. But most importantly, the fight cannot occur during normal business hours. Can't have someone like me interfering with the precious cogs in your precious machinery, can you? Therefore, at five OH ONE pm today," Saru tossed the scroll over the mayor's face, "I will untie your mayor and beat the piss out of him on teleblimp. And then I'll become the mayor."

"Hot dogs!" Nick shouted. "If he becomes the mayor, then, then—"

"The city is doomed?"

"No! I'll *never* get my business license. Unless—" Kanna clenched a fist. "We stop him?"

"No, I was thinking—"

Saru patted the mayor on his scroll-covered head. "In a few hours, you'll all be calling me . . . hizzoner. *Au revoir*, dipshits." The massive screen went black.

Nick glared at the blimp. "Fucking blimps."

"Yes, I get it, they're assholes. Come on, let's get to the safe house. We'll track Saru from there." Kanna strode across the rooftop.

"I'm not coming."

That stopped her. "What?"

"I'm going to go see the deputy mayor. I'm sure there's some clause that makes him acting mayor if the actual mayor gets kidnapped by ninjas. He can sign my license." Nick waved the sheaf of papers, then figured that looked kind of condescending, like *of course* she knows what a business license is, she clearly would've needed one for the Clan Hanasu Nezumi Ninjutsu/CrossFit Academy, so he shoved them back in his pocket.

"Nick, this is bigger than your business license. This is Kundarai Saru we're talking about. We can finally get revenge!"

"Revenge, Kanna? It's my fault the master—" Nick's words caught in his throat, he turned and coughed into his hand, hoping by the time he finished Kanna would have moved on to a different topic. Like woodworking, or professional rugby.

"Nick."

He looked up. Kanna was standing close, very close. She usually only got that close to her victims. She put a hand on his cheek. Her palm felt smooth and warm. Brought back some old feelings, long forgotten.

Ninja magic.

"I need your help, Nick. I've been hunting Saru for years, and every time he's slipped through my fingers. Worse, he's grown more powerful. Rumor is he's mastered the Sticks of Heaven."

Nick gaped at her. "That's impossible! No one since Orenji-iro—"

"I know. But if there's any truth to it—"

50

"Then there's nothing either of us can do. Except open up a drive-thru fondue restaurant. And whatever you're planning on doing. Ever thought about getting your real estate license?"

Kanna shoved him, hard.

Nick staggered back, slipping on gravel.

"Dammit, Nick, I haven't seen you in ten years and all you can talk about is fondue? Sticks or no Sticks, if we work together Saru won't stand a chance against us. I'm the daughter of Makoto Kikuchi. And you, you're the *Chosen One*."

"That was a long time ago."

"The past is never far behind us."

Nick turned away. "Call the rest of Clan Hanasu Nezumi. They'll fight with you."

"They did."

"What do you—"

"He killed them, Nick. All of them." Kanna's steady voice wavered, a slight hitch marring her speech. Her beautiful brown eyes glistened in the mid-morning sun.

Nick's stomach seized up. All of them? His friends, the ninjas he'd grown up with? The kids he'd played baseball with, and *Street Fighter?* Snuck into Van Damme movies? Those same kids?

Something the master said to him came back. Not the ninja one, the fondue one. Old Pierre. "We are all like the melting fromage. Our memories, our experiences, all become a single, delicious slurry. Oh, merde, you've burned the bread again!"

He smiled at the memory. Now there was one master he hadn't killed, and maybe his words of wisdom weren't directly applicable to Nick's current situation, but he did know one thing.

You can melt a wedge of cheese.

But you can't unmelt it.

A police helicopter zoomed by, then circled back. "You, on the roof!" a mechanical voice squawked.

"I'm sorry, Kanna," Nick said, turning away.

"I'm sorry, too," Kanna said softly.

They jumped off the roof, headed in very different directions.

Neither noticing the ninja on another rooftop, half a mile away, watching them intently through binoculars.

AN AUDIENCE WITH THE DEPUTY MAYOR

OTHER THAN THE fleet of police, fire and rescue vehicles, the yellow tape, the panicked crowds, the gaggle of reporters shouting questions, the rancid stink of blood, the sheet-draped bodies being carried out the front door on stretchers, and the work crew pulling down the old statue of Mayor DiFormaggio because *of course* that bitch-assed bitch was going to get his ass handed to him, City Hall looked basically the same as it had earlier that morning when Nick was merely a simple aspiring small businessman, fresh from a fight with a gang of street toughs and sweating his balls off from a four-mile run.

He slipped his bloody jacket back on and headed to the entrance, trying once again to look like a super-serious business guy. Maybe he even did, Nick didn't know much about the business world but he figured those guys probably came home covered in blood at least a couple times a month.

The entrance to City Hall was taped off. A squat policeman who looked like a fireplug directed traffic. Nick approached, making a mental note to figure out what the fuck a *fireplug* was. Maybe he'd ask Rondell, dude knew everything.

"Excuse me, sir, this is a crime scene," the officer said.

Lying didn't come easily to Nick, but he tried anyway. "I've got an appointment with the deputy mayor." He checked his watch. "For 10:30."

"The deputy mayor's busy, kid," the officer replied, indicating the chaotic scene around them with the sweep of a hand.

"But I have an appointment."

The cop eyed him, then shrugged. "What do I care? I got five more hours until retirement." He lifted the crime scene tape and motioned Nick under.

"Thanks," Nick said, ducking under the tape and heading inside the building. He didn't hear the workers shout LOOK OUT, or see the massive statue of Mayor Joe DiFormaggio coming loose, and he definitely didn't notice when said statue keeled over and squashed the almost-retired cop.

The scene inside was equally chaotic. Nick looked around for someone who could help him. "Excuse me," he said to a pair of official-looking folks squatting on the floor, "where's the deputy mayor's office?"

The EMT looked up from giving mouth-to-mouth to an older blonde woman with a rather nasty sai wound in one of her fake tits, said, "Second floor, end of the hall," then resumed her task.

Nick headed back to the stairwell. This time, he didn't hear any muffled thumps or screams, so he took that as a sign maybe, just maybe, he could get his business license signed, and then he and Rondell could go out for a celebratory milkshake to commemorate the fact that Fond Dudes was no longer a twinkle in their collective eyes, but a real, concrete liquified cheese concern.

The door to the second floor opened quietly. Unlike the chaotic third floor, the second was clean and orderly. Lights flickered softly overhead. He wandered down the hallway, checking the stencils on the doors. Comptroller. City Attorney. Chief Bikini Inspector.

And finally, Deputy Mayor.

Nick knocked. No one answered. "Mr. or Mrs. Deputy Mayor? My name's Nick. I have some papers for you to sign. *Business* papers."

Still no answer. He knocked again, then poked his head in the door. "Hello?"

The deputy mayor's office was dark. Dust and cobwebs covered everything. It didn't look very professional, but then again the actual mayor had a broken window and a dead guy lying on the bloody carpet, so Nick shouldn't have been too surprised.

A slight figure sat behind the desk, still, unmoving.

Nick took a few steps into the office. "Uh, hi, I'm sure you're busy, I wanted to see if you could sign my business license and then I'll be on my way. It's for a restaurant my friend and I are opening. Uh, best friend, actually." Nick nodded to himself, thinking that was a pretty professional explanation which totally merited a quick signature.

The deputy mayor said nothing.

"Hey, are you okay?" Nick asked. He took another step closer.

And froze.

The deputy mayor wasn't sitting behind the desk, he was sitting *on* the desk. Maybe a foot and a half tall. He stared back at Nick, stony-faced. Nick quickly ran back the last thirty seconds to see if he'd accidentally said something untoward about little people, who certainly made for as capable civic employees as tallfolk in Nick's estimation, but he couldn't think of anything he might have said to cause offense.

Then the light shifted and he realized the deputy mayor wasn't angry at all.

He'd just been carved that way.

The crude eyebrows and abruptly-tilting mustache gave the statue a permanent scowl. Nick considered himself a pretty friendly and outgoing guy, but even he couldn't think of anything to say that might win over an inanimate object. Plus, the deputy mayor's hands were carved into his body, so even if he miraculously gained sentience through a lightning strike or some other bit of '80s teen comedy chicanery, he wouldn't be signing any business licenses now or ever.

Nick's heart sank.

His dream was dead.

Might as well forsake my vow altogether, go back to Japan, pick up some freelance ninja work.

Maybe, if he was lucky, some Yakuza punk would put a 9mm round through Nick's stupid, loser forehead.

Feeling more alone than when he'd first fled to Europe in the bowels of a tramp steamer, with only a crate of off-brand DVD players with their bullshit

Region 2 coding for company, Nick trudged down the stairs, past a crew of workers desperately trying to get the statue off the smushed fireplug cop, and back through Kersey Park, headed for his studio apartment and the sullen, solitary existence awaiting him. When a different gang of street toughs predictably accosted him, he barely felt the baseball bats, chains, and two-by-fours crashing into his back and shoulders.

Eventually they got bored and went off to look for an assault victim who'd actually give a shit about his vicious beating.

VILLAINOUS GLOATING/MEET THE HENCHMEN

"**AND THAT'S A WRAP!**" Saru clapped his hands together, leering at the mayor. The current and not-much-longer Hizzoner looked so catatonic they hardly needed the duct tape. His eyes stared blankly, a damp stain spreading at his crotch.

Saru's nose twitched at the heady, vinegar scent. "Ew, gross. Daisuke?"

His right-hand ninja materialized in front of him, wearing his usual red, long-nosed Tengu mask over his shinobi shōzoku. "Yes, master?"

"Get that loser out of my sight. Now."

"Hai!"

Daisuke bowed, motioned at two ninja trainees. They grabbed the mayor by his duct-taped feet and hauled him away.

Saru shook his head. "What a mook. Okay, get the others, we've got work to do."

Daisuke stuck two fingers in his mouth and whistled.

NUNCHUCK CITY

The ground swayed beneath Saru's feet, a loud belch erupted from the doorway. Most of it was occupied by Slag Cromwell, the once-famous gaijin sumo. A mountain of a man, the wrestler's career was brought to an ignominious end by a rare gastro-intestinal disease which necessitated the removal of his lower intestine and the addition of a colostomy bag. Slag appealed, but the JSA wasn't about to let a sumo with a biohazard bomb strapped to his waist into the ring. After that he drifted into the Tokyo underworld, snapping necks and backs for the Yakuza. Until his particular branch of ninkyō dantai ran afoul of Saru. Slag switched sides, the rest was ninja history.

"You called, boss?" Slag said in his heavy Australian accent. He was wearing a keshō-mawashi that showed off his colostomy bag, his ample stomach, and the nasty case of psoriasis he'd developed as of late. He'd also added a pair of spiked leather gauntlets to his ensemble. Saru had lost a half-dozen ninjas to various puncture wounds over the last week.

"Yes," Saru said. "Where's—"

Silent as her namesake, Sasayaku flipped down from the ceiling next to Daisuke, wearing a deep purple yoroi. She never wore a mask—some might have thought it vanity, a stubborn refusal to deny the world her exquisite cheekbones, but Saru knew it was so her face would be the last thing her victims ever saw. A creature of rage and fury, seeking not admiration but blood. Sasayaku smirked and sparked her tekagi-shuko, tiger hand claws, against one another.

Saru regarded his lieutenants. The most powerful warriors in the world, all gathered together to do his bidding. A lesser man might have feared such vipers would one day turn on their master, and while he entertained the thought, he did not fear it—he welcomed it.

They were nothing to him, so long as he possessed the Sticks of Heaven.

"You've done well, so far," Saru said. "But though our first prize is in our grasp, we cannot rest. There's much to do."

Slag grinned. Daisuke and Sasayaku didn't react at all.

"Undoubtedly, the remaining authorities will attempt a rescue. Your job, Slag, is to sow disorder. Take a contingent of ninja and attack the city. Smash, burn, destroy! In other words, what you do best."

"Oi!" Slag shouted, and disappeared back through the doorway.

"Daisuke, you'll hit police headquarters. Annihilate their leadership, their communications."

Daisuke bowed, left the room.

"Sasayaku, I've got a very special job for you. The mayor is not our only interest in Turbo City. There's power here, power I would make my own. Take a small force and—"

The walkie-talkie in his kimono squawked. "Master?"

"One moment." Saru pulled out the walkie-talkie. "Yes?"

"We've got a problem. The last daughter of Clan Hanasu Nezumi, she is here! In Turbo City."

"I know where we are, idiot." Saru turned to

NUNCHUCK CITY

Sasayaku. "Complete your primary objective. And when you have finished, scour the city for Kanna Kikuchi. Bring her to me. Alive, or—" Saru shrugged.

Sasayaku's normally-impassive face broke into a wide grin. "As you will, master. As you fucking will."

TOTAL BITCH MOVES

NICK PUSHED OPEN the door to his apartment, which now seemed bathed in a sickly, sallow glow because he'd forgotten to open the windows. But also because depression. A rare, foreign feeling in Nick—despite all the ups and downs of his life, his self-imposed exile, the long winter days spent trudging up and down a mountain in the French Alps at the behest of Pierre, he remained a pretty upbeat guy.

Until now.

Flopping on the futon, Nick pressed a throw pillow over his face, blocking out the world, or at least his super-depressing apartment. He wondered how long he'd be able to afford it. Maybe he could go back to slinging fondue on the streets. But how could he take a step back like that?

Eyes bored into him from across the room.

Nick tossed the pillow aside, slogged over to the framed portrait of Pierre by the nightstand, and turned it to face the wall. He couldn't let any of his various masters see him like this, but especially Pierre.

The phone rang.

Like most ninjas, Nick didn't carry a cell—one buzz

at an inopportune time might reveal your position to the enemy, and even though he didn't think of himself as a ninja anymore, old habits die hard. Nick was one of twelve people in all of Turbo City who had a landline, and the youngest by at least forty years.

Nick eyed the phone, wondering if he should answer it, or go back to moping on the futon. He couldn't imagine it was good news. Unless maybe the city clerk had unilaterally decided because of the extenuating circumstances of the mayor getting kidnapped and the deputy mayor being an inanimate object, she'd waive the requirement to have his business license signed. But Nick couldn't imagine her giving that much of a shit.

He let the answering machine get it.

"Hey there, friend! You've reached the answering machine of Nick Nikolopoulos. There's going to be this beep thing, and then you want to leave a message. A message is a communication detailing who you are, why you're calling, and where I might be able to reach you. A communication is a verbal or written message. Obviously verbal in this case. Hope that makes sense. I'm pretty new at this. I spent the last few years in the French Al—BEEP."

"Nick, you there?"

Rondell.

Nick glanced at the window, thought about throwing himself through it. But that wouldn't solve anything. He'd always faced his problems head-on, whether they came in the form of a rival ninja clan trying to chop his ass into bite-size pieces or a mystical fox spirit that had gotten stuck inside an illustrated book about Japanese birds.

And maybe telling his best friend the mutual dream they'd harbored for several weeks was dead would be difficult, but it couldn't compare to trying to convince a panicked fox spirit to stop chasing Okinawa woodpeckers and recite a summoning incantation backwards, damn it!

"Anyway," Rondell continued, "I'm calling—"

Nick snatched the phone out of its cradle. "Hey, Rondell."

"Nick! What's the word?"

"Just got back," Nick said, pulling the unfulfilled business license from his pocket.

"And?"

Nick glanced down at the blank signature line. *Mayor,* it screamed back at him. *Mayor, dipshit!*

"Did you hear what happened at City Hall?"

"You know I don't follow politics. Tell me the license is all squared away, because I've got news!"

Nick blinked. "News?"

"You're not going to believe it. Turns out my cousin, Trevor? He knows the touring bassist for C+C Music Factory. I pulled some strings and they've agreed to play our opening as long as it's this Tuesday from three o'clock to three-fifteen!"

Nick almost dropped the phone. "What?"

"Look, I know they're like one of two bands you listened to growing up, so I couldn't pass up the opportunity to have them play our grand opening!"

Tuesday was mere days away. The four walls of his apartment closed in around Nick, which wasn't hard because the whole room was like 8x10. Inches. He usually used a sheet of loose-leaf paper for carpet because that was an extra twenty-five bucks a month.

"Nick? You there?"

"Yeah, I'm here!"

"Okay, so we're good on the license?"

Nick held the phone away, staring out his window at the brick wall across the street. "We're . . . good."

Oh, nooooo.

"Great, I'll text you the details. Wait, you don't have a cell. Maybe I'll get a carrier pigeon or some shit. Smoke signals, I dunno, I'll figure it out, that's on me. The important thing is, we're in business! Fond Dudes for life, right?"

Nick's mouth went dry. What the hell had he just done? Lied, for one, something he never did. His old master, the ninja one, used to say, "Lies are the nut punches of conversation." Total bitch moves.

Had he just made a bitch move?

"Fond Dudes for life," Nick croaked, and hung up. He slumped back down on the futon, head in hands, the unsigned business license fluttering to the floor. What was he going to do?

Nick curled up into a very un-ninja-like (or master fondue chef-like, for that matter) fetal position. His eyes watered, he stifled a sob. Rondell was going to be so disappointed in him. Not to mention C+C Music Factory. How could he possibly face the surviving and replacement members of the band who'd crafted such seminal hits as "Gonna Make you Sweat (Everybody Dance Now)" and, well, he didn't know any of their other songs, but the Inter-Dojo Ninja Sock Hop was one of his fondest childhood memories, and—

Nick sat bolt upright. Maybe he hadn't dug himself into a friendship hole, after all. Maybe he was really building a friendship TOWER. One consisting of him, Rondell—

And Kanna.

After all, it wasn't *really* a lie if he did the thing he said he was going to, was it?

He glanced at his watch. Almost noon. Five hours to find Kundarai Saru and stop him from beating the ever-loving shit out of the mayor.

But first, Nick needed to find Kanna.

Scratch that.

First, Nick needed to fucking change.

WHO THE FUCK IS IN CHARGE HERE, ANYWAY?

DEEP BENEATH CITY HALL, in a cavern crowned by dripping stalactites, at a long, ebony table, the real powers that ran Turbo City convened and played with their smart phones.

LINDSEY BRECKENRIDGE, City Attorney.

DOUG FREDERSON, Water and Sewage Manager.

LAKSHMI RAO, CEO of Turbo Tech, the city's largest employer and maker of cool shit with circuits and flashing lights and whatnot.

And finally—

CHAD BONER, Chief Bikini Inspector.

Chad Boner put down his Ceremonial Magnifying Glass and picked up his Ceremonial Emergency Gavel.

BANG!

"Bros and brosettes, let this meeting of the Turbo

City Auxiliary Council totally come to order. I will not mince words, or waste time ogling your very fine breasts. Turbo City is in crisis. Things haven't been this bad since Four Loko stopped putting caffeine in its high-quality alcoholic beverages. It is up to us to set things right. That is my opening statement. Penis."

"Your honor—" Lindsey Breckenridge began.

Lakshmi Rao cleared her throat. "Um, Madame Attorney, I believe the appropriate honorific is Dr. Tits McGee."

"Who cares? Some ninja asshole's kidnapped the mayor, we've got to do something."

Doug raised a hand. "Why don't we call the governor? Have her send in the National Guard?"

Everyone rolled their eyes.

"We can't do that, Shitboy," Chad Boner said. "We'll look like total pussies if they find out our mayor's been kidnapped. Can you even imagine what those chumps in Xtremington will say?"

"Fucking Xtremington," Lindsey Breckinridge muttered, curling her perfectly-manicured fingers into a tight fist.

"They won't be *saying* anything," Lakshmi Rao said. "Turbo Tech has already shut down communications to the outside world. Nobody's going to find out our dirty little secret. Yet."

Chad Boner gave her a fist bump. "Radical. So, we've got some time." He turned to Lindsey. "What are we hearing from the police?"

"I dunno, was I supposed to call them?"

"You're the city attorney!"

"So?"

"It's related!"

Doug raised another hand. "I can call Chief Yang."

"Like he wants to talk to you, Shitboy," Lakshmi Rao said, sending a return fist bump Chad Boner's way.

"Huh-huh, nice one," Chad Boner said, sniffing his knuckles and closing his eyes.

"Quick break so Chad and I can smash?" Lakshmi asked.

"We don't *have* twenty seconds, Lakshmi," the City Attorney said.

"Fine, I'll finger-bang her under the table until we're done," Chad Boner said, reaching across Doug's lap and sliding a hand up Lakshmi's skirt. The CEO gasped, then leaned back in her chair, eyes shut, a placid expression spreading on her face.

The slight rhythm see-sawing across Doug's pleated khakis was simultaneously frightening and distracting. He scooched his chair away from the table and tripped over a stalagmite.

"Yo, Linds, you want some of this? I got a spare," Chad asked, wiggling the fingers on his free hand.

"No, you fucking don't," Lakshmi said, grabbing his wrist and pulling it down into her lap. A massive groan escaped her lips.

Doug picked himself up off the cavern floor. "I'm going to go call the chief. And maybe get this looked at." He held up his palm, a bloody, glory hole-sized wound punched through the middle.

"Take it sleazy, Shitboy," Chad Boner called over his shoulder, using both of his fists to their maximum advantage underneath the table. Lakshmi grabbed him by the ears and screamed into his face.

"While we've got a quorum, should we give ourselves raises?" Lindsey Breckinridge asked.

"Good idea," Chad Boner said, offering her a very moist and gooey fist bump.

Lindsey declined.

ASSHOLE NINJA HUNT

KANNA SPREAD THE map wide over the kitchen table in her safe house, took a step back, and frowned.

Where the fuck was this dickhead at?

Turbo City was huge, and she didn't know it at all. She'd only been to the States a few times. Ninja work kept her mostly confined to Japan and Hong Kong, although one time she'd been contracted to shoot a tenor in the balls with a beanbag shotgun during a performance at the Sydney Opera House, so he could hit the high note at just the right moment.

Kanna picked up a red magic marker and tentatively waved it over the map. Kundarai Saru was a ghost. One thing he was very good at, acting like a massive piece of shit being the other. When he'd first arrived at her clan's dojo with his lanky limbs and stank-ass attitude, her father took one look at the former software inventor and said, "Henceforth, you shall be called Kudaranai Saru."

Kanna tried her best not to laugh. Luckily, she was rocking a shinobi shōzoku at the time so homeboy couldn't see her twitchy-ass grin.

"What's that mean?" the guy who was now named Saru asked.

"It means," her father said, speaking slowly, "Glorious Warrior."

She damn near pissed her ninja-pants.

"Wow, Kundarai Saru," Saru said, already grievously mis-pronouncing his new name. "And I haven't even punched anybody yet." He wandered wide-eyed into the dojo.

Her father shot her a wry smile. "Sorry, couldn't resist."

Kanna snorted. "But what happens when he learns Japanese? He's going to find out you named him Shitty Monkey."

"That one will *never* learn Japanese."

And outside of a few odd phrases he used to convey his various kinks to the local prostitutes ("O shiri o yubi de agete kudasai!" or "Finger up the butt, please!" being one notable example), he never did.

Normally, her father would never take on a student so obviously guaranteed to eventually bring shame on their dojo, but they were desperate for money and Saru was a former tech douchebag. Her father could charge him a hundred times the usual rate for advanced ninjutsu instruction and he wouldn't even blink an eye.

They just had to put up with him.

Predictably, Saru ended up screwing them over, using his newfound ninjutsu skills to brutalize innocents and construct a criminal empire to rival the Yakuza. For the past decade, Kanna chased him all over the globe, never quite catching him. When she'd run into Nick after so many years, her gut told her perhaps she'd finally get her long-sought revenge. Fate had brought them back together.

But Nick was a shadow of himself. A cheese-melter who could barely fight. She was wrong to think things could be different.

This Nick? The Turbo City Nick?

Motherfucker would end up getting them both killed.

A shadow passed by the front window of the apartment. Kanna grabbed her ninjato, the blade gleaming in the midday light, and circled across the room, avoiding the windows in case they had guns.

Whoever *they* were.

Boards creaked outside her door. She approached, ninjato held low at her side. A single thrust through the door would eliminate the threat. She listened for the sounds of slides racking, swords being drawn from scabbards, shuriken clinking together.

KNOCK-KNOCK!

"Kanna?" Nick's muffled voice called. "You in there?"

Kanna gaped at the door. He'd managed to find her safehouse. Maybe the old Nick was still in there, somewhere.

She slipped the ninjato into its scabbard and opened the door. Nick stood there, smiling awkwardly. Unlike the last time she'd seen him, he looked much more like himself—white jeans, black tank top, scuffed combat boots. He wore black leather fingerless gloves on each hand, and a black bandana wrapped around his head like a hachimaki. And despite ten years of pacifism and French cooking, he still retained the same lean muscle tone she'd always found irresistible. If there was something of the old Nick still inside of him, there was certainly something of the old Kanna inside herself, and the old Kanna wanted very badly to grab him by the bandana and drag him into the bedroom.

Maybe after they found Saru and beat the ever-loving shit out of him.

"How'd you find me?" Kanna asked.

Nick shrugged. "Went back to where we parted, tracked you to this building. Then I knocked on every door until I found you."

That was Nick, all right. Maybe not the smoothest operator, but definitely the stubbornest. And sometimes, brute force was exactly what the ninja doctor ordered. "I'm glad you came."

Nick looked down, scratching the back of his neck. "Yeah. So, uh, can I come in?"

"Oh, of course!" Kanna felt slightly embarrassed she'd let Nick linger there by the front door. She moved to the side, letting him enter. As he passed, she caught a whiff of cologne. Her heart raced at the scent. She shook her head slightly, pushed the door closed.

Nick examined the map on the kitchen table. "Got any leads on Saru?"

"I thought you didn't care about Saru. What changed your mind?"

He looked her in the eye. "Realized I can't leave my friends hanging. Old friends, or new ones."

"Thanks." They were silent for a moment, inches from each other, and Kanna kind of wanted to touch him, lay a hand on his arm, but she didn't, and then the moment passed and she pointed at the map. "You know this place better than I do. Any idea where Saru might be holed up?"

Nick's finger drew circles on the map. "Can't be

more than a few miles from City Hall, the broadcast started pretty quickly. What do we know about Saru?"

"He's a dick?"

"Other than that."

"He sneezes weird. Like, really loud. Um." Squeezing the bridge of her nose, Kanna struggled to remember anything else that might be useful. She'd kept her distance from Saru as much as possible, because in addition to his shitty attitude he was also really handsy, and her father explicitly told her not to brutally murder him until Saru signed over all his financial holdings. Over the last decade, she'd learned little about him. Saru appeared in random cities, beat up all the local martial arts teachers, and usually robbed a museum or some shit. He didn't seem to care about much besides money and power.

Think, girl, think—

"Um, he likes Ethiopian food."

Nick circled the Addis Ababa House, Chez Addis Ababa, and a weed store called Ethidopia just in case. "What else?"

"Karaoke?"

"He does do a pretty decent Barry White. Anything else?" Nick frowned, pointed at a newspaper on the counter. "Is that today's edition?"

"Yep." Kanna grabbed the paper and unfurled it, eyeing the headline. "Martial Arts Maven Maimed by Mysterious Malefactor? Jesus, that's a lot of alliteration."

Nick tapped the ass-end of the marker against the table. "Here." He circled an address in a neighborhood called Agave Gardens, near the extreme southern edge of the map.

"The scene of the crime? Nick, Saru's long gone."

Nick drew a red line from the Agave Gardens address across the map. "Not there." He turned to Kanna, grinning. "The closest hospital."

OH SHIT, REMEMBER THIS DUDE???

THE MOST DANGEROUS Man in Turbo City had definitely seen better days. Nick and Kanna watched from the doorway of Skip Baxter's hospital room while a nurse took his vitals. Baxter looked like a snowman, everything from his Feet of Fury™ to his Deadly Weapons™ sealed up in a full-body cast. Tubes snaked this way and that, various machines beeped and blorped. The room smelled of convalescence and antiseptic.

The nurse finished and brushed past them. "He's all yours."

"You go," Kanna said, nudging Nick in the ribs.

Nick approached the bed. "Mr. Baxter?"

The man's eyes flicked towards Nick. "My son. You came."

"Uh, I'm Nick. This is Kanna."

"Why, hello—"

"Mr. Baxter," Nick said. "Tell us what happened."

The little slice of Skip-face they could see went red. "My sworn enemy ambushed me. In my own dojo!"

"No way him and Saru ever met before," Kanna whispered.

"And?" Nick prompted.

"We fought! An epic battle that shook the heavens. I gave it my all, but—"

Kanna picked up the chart posted on the end of his bed. "No defensive wounds, I see."

Nick elbowed her. "I'm sure you put up a valiant fight."

"Damn tootin'. But even I, Skip Baxter, am no match for . . . evil ninja magic."

"There's literally no such thing," Kanna said.

"Kundy Ricey Roo is a practitioner of the black arts!" Skip cried. "The power he wields is . . . unfathomable."

"Yes, the power to punch you in the face a bunch of times," Kanna said. "Clearly supernatural."

"Must have been magic. No way a guy with a voice like that could have taken me."

Nick wandered over to the window. Up in the sky, the teleblimp circled, preparing to simul-cast Saru's impending mayoral ass-kicking, mere hours away. He didn't know what they were going to do. This Skip Baxter guy was a dead end, he couldn't tell them where Saru was hiding out. The guy was a poser who knew approximately fuck-all about martial arts. Chances are the whole experience was a blur.

Nick sighed, turned back to the hospital bed. "Mr. Baxter, can you remember anything Kundarai Saru might have said?"

Skip tried to shake his head. Screamed until the nurse stuck her head in and said, "Cut it out, some people here are in actual pain." She looked at Kanna and said, "Mr. Baxter *insisted* on the cast."

"I like her," Kanna said.

"Let's go," Nick said, heading for the door. "We need a new plan. Maybe we can draw Saru out. Somehow."

"We can try the Ethiopian restaurants. Saru might've gotten delivery. And if not, let's hit the karaoke bars. Always a chance he's killing time until—" Kanna spun, rushed over to Skip's bed. "What did you say? About his voice?"

"He sounded like a pussy. Real high voice, a soprano."

Nick frowned. "Saru doesn't have a high voice. He always did—"

"Barry White, karaoke night!" Kanna finished.

"Weird. Why would his voice be high?"

Kanna shrugged. "Maybe he got drunk and chopped his own balls off. Guys do that, right?"

"Pretty much never. But—" Nick pulled the map out of his pocket and spread it across Skip's cast-covered body, "—that gives me an idea. What's inside of a blimp?"

Kanna's eyes went wide. "Helium!"

"He's at the airfield." Nick re-folded the map, he and Kanna headed for the door.

"Avenge me, my son!" Skip called after them.

Then broke down sobbing.

DR. POOP, PH.D.

IF THERE'S ONE THING Doug Frederson knew, it was shit.

Not metaphorical shit—his life was relatively trouble-free. Played fullback in high school. Earned a bachelor's in engineering. Married his high school sweetheart, Betty. Got a job with the city, had some kids, coached soccer on Thursdays and took his still-lovely wife out to dinner at the Crêpes of Wrath on Fridays. Grilled, mowed the lawn, lived the shit.

Bowled a perfect game, once.

A good life. A quiet life. So Doug Frederson, the kind of shit he knew?

Real shit.

Actual shit.

Poop, if you will.

Except that moment, walking into the police station and seeing nary a soul?

Doug Frederson suddenly knew both kinds of shit. And it scared him.

"Hello?" Doug called. "It's Doug. Frederson. From the Water Department?"

That was Doug's thing. Half his title was *water,* the other half *sewage,* and all anybody ever cared about was the last part. Some unfunny asshole dad would waddle up to him after a soccer game and go, "So you're the shit guy? Must be pretty *shitty* work!" Doug started introducing himself as the head of the Water Department, not the Water and Sewage Department, and nobody cared except that horrid woman Lindsey Breckinridge, or that douchebag Chad Boner. Lakshmi Rao wouldn't give him the time of day, which was a sure step up from the non-stop splurting sewer pipe of poop jokes the other asshole members of the Secret Council farted his way. Doug wasn't a guy who hated things, he spent half his time elbows-deep in diarrhea for Chrissakes, but he was awful close to H-A-single crucifix-E hating those Secret Council meetings.

And yet, somebody had to do the actual work of running Turbo City, besides Rhonda.

Doug was a guy who *never* shirked his duty. Or his doody. Just wasn't in his DNA.

Which is what brought him to an empty police station.

"Hello?" Doug tried again, voice echoing. He walked over to the desk, extended a hand to ding the bell—

Something, some primal impulse surviving even in portly sewage-managing Thursday night soccer coaches, told him not to. Not to make a fucking sound.

Doug swallowed hard, sweat running rampant down his lower back, backed away from the desk quietly as he could.

The floor groaned under his feet.

Doug cursed the truly amazing meatball sandwich he'd had for second breakfast. Cautiously looked, listened, for any sign of whatever was nattering his Dougey-senses.

Somewhere far, far in the back of the station, maybe even in Chief Yang's office—

Metal scraped against bone.

Doug turned tail, burst through the double doors, and fell down the steps. Behind him, he could sense a still, calm presence—perversely calm—standing silently over whatever grim task it had been about and listening for his water-and-sewage managing ass.

The sidewalk was as bizarrely empty as the station itself.

Doug dusted off his khakis, glanced back at the station. Any minute, something was going to come bursting through those doors. Something that hated city employees, perfect-game bowlers, and men named Doug with enlarged prostates that aren't necessarily a concern yet, but kind of concern*ing* for a guy your age, just something to keep an eye on, okay, champ?

Doug looked about desperately, hoping all the cops had been at a team-building event in Kersey Park and were now coming back from a delightful lunch hour filled with trust falls, secret circles, and friendship walks.

Ha. Fucking nobody, man.

With the police station pulsing malignantly in front of him, and no one coming to his rescue, Doug did the one thing that made sense.

He nearly threw out his back yanking up a manhole cover.

And dove into the sewer.

OH COME ON, IT'S A FUCKING HOSPITAL FOR CHRISSAKES

NICK AND KANNA exited Turbo City Presbyterian. An ambulance screeched up and disgorged a couple EMTs and a very bloody woman strapped to a stretcher. They rolled her into the ER. Another ambulance pulled up behind the first one. In the distance, more sirens wailed, promising a never-ending repetition of the same scene they'd just witnessed.

"Geez," Nick said. "Busy day at the hospital."

"It's Saru. His ninjas are running roughshod over the city. Attacking people for sport."

"What a dick." Nick checked his watch. "We've only got a couple hours left. We should get to the airfield."

"Okay, I'll drive." They headed for the six-story concrete parking structure where they'd left Kanna's rental, a late model RAV4. Not exactly a ninja car, but no cars were ninja cars. Ninjas flipped their way across the landscape, swung from grappling hooks, caught rides (and had kick-ass fights) on top of trains. In a pinch, they'd get on a motorcycle.

They did *not* drive mid-size sport utility vehicles.

Nick dug the parking ticket out of his pants. "Should I go see if they'll validate this at the front desk?"

"No time."

"It's fifteen bucks."

"It's okay, I've got it."

Nick was still pretty shocked he'd run into Kanna after all these years, she wasn't mad at him for killing her father, *and* she had fifteen dollars. Maybe this was a sign. Things were going to work out after all.

Yet another ambulance peeled into the parking lot, narrowly missing them. Once again, the back doors opened and EMTs jumped out, pushing a sheet-draped body on a gurney.

"That doesn't look good," Nick said. "Poor gu—"

The body suddenly shot up, the sheet flying away to reveal a black-clad ninja. The EMTs grabbed Uzis off the gurney and spun, firing wildly at Nick and Kanna, while the ninja backflipped on top of the ambulance, pointing at them with a long naginata.

BRRRRRRRRRRRRRRRAPPPPPPPPPPPPP!

Kanna tackled Nick, pulling him behind a post. Bullets dinged off the pillar, filling the air with concrete dust.

Nick coughed. "Guess Saru's onto us."

"Yeah. That dick." Kanna pulled her manriki. "You want the Uzi losers or the naga-nimrod?"

The ninja appeared behind them, naginata pointed at Nick.

"Ninja!" Nick yelled, spearing the ninja. He slammed into the man, pancaking him into the cement. The naginata went flying, stuck in a Beamer's

84

tire. Incredibly expensive European air departed with a *whoosh*.

"Fine, take the guy who doesn't have a gun," Kanna said somewhere behind them.

Nick slammed an elbow into the ninja's face, the impact reverberating up his shoulder. The ninja's head smacked against the pavement.

Nick reared back with another elbow, but the ninja kneed him in the taint. Pain exploded throughout his groin. He groaned, rolled off.

The ninja sprung to his feet, but wavered—maybe concussed from all that sweet, sweet elbow music. Pulled a small dagger from the depths of his tunic.

Somewhere out in the parking lot, Uzis barked like incredibly aggressive chihuahuas. BRRRRAPPP, BRRRAPPP, BRR—

"Argh!" Someone—definitely not Kanna—screamed.

Nick gritted his teeth and stood, the pain already subsiding. During all his years of training, both to become a ninja and then a fondue chef, he'd felt far worse.

The ninja danced forward, slicing the air with the dagger. Nick stutter-stepped back, then threw some punches, but the ninja weaved out of reach. Nick waited for him to advance again, then kicked him in the chest, knocking him back. The ninja crashed into a Jag, smashing the sideview mirror.

"Come on!" Nick yelled.

The ninja lunged again, the blade biting into Nick's forearm.

Shallow. A scratch.

But a warning.

Next cut might be something important.

Nick feinted, danced back. The ninja didn't bite, circling patiently, knife swishing the air.

Another burst of gunfire rang out, spackling the tail-ends of parked cars, shattering glass.

Nick honed in on the naginata, sticking out of the deflated tire of the Beamer. Right behind the ninja.

The ninja charged. Nick ran at him, tensing his knees at the last second and springing over his attacker. He landed on his hands, sprang off the ground and nailed the ninja in the back with both feet. The ninja crashed into a concrete pillar with a loud *whumph*.

The naginata lay mere feet from Nick.

He scrabbled across the ground, grabbed the handle and wrenched the spear free, spinning to meet his attacker. The ninja, whoozy from his face-first collision, turned and tossed the knife from hand to hand.

"Come on," Nick snarled.

The ninja flipped the knife to his right hand, tossed it at Nick. Everything slowed down. The tip of the knife sailed towards Nick's face.

He swung the naginata, knocking the knife away. It sailed across the parking garage, severing the truck nutz off an F-150.

"Hai!" the ninja yelled, tossing a pair of smoke bombs. A thick cloud of smoke engulfed Nick, filling his mouth, his throat, with brimstone stench. He coughed, dropped to a crouch, eyes burning. Moved in a circle, careful of errant shadows materializing out of the thick, pungent cloud.

Nick closed his eyes.

Tears still streamed down his cheeks, but the burning lessened. He listened, at first only to his own breathing, muted gunfire and screams outside the parking garage.

Then he heard it.

A single heartbeat, at his six.

Nick thrust.

A slight resistance, a quiet *shunk,* a louder *oh* spilled out of the lips of the ninja.

Nick opened his eyes.

The smoke was already dissipating. He'd impaled the ninja, run him straight through the heart with the naginata. The man dangled on the spear, limbs slack, blood bubbling from the wound, nearly invisible against his dark shinobi shōzoku.

Nick let him fall to the ground, where he twitched a few times and then moved no more.

"Sorry," Nick muttered, turning away from the dead man. He never liked this part much, but the guy didn't give him much of a choice.

"DIE, MOTHERFUCKER!"

Nick whirled. An EMT leveled an Uzi at him. The man's grin stretched wide, like he was jacked on Benzedrine, like the old kamikazes.

The EMT squeezed the trigger.

Kanna's manriki whished out of nowhere, wrapping around the man's throat and spinning him away. Bullets ripped into the ceiling, sprayed parked cars, shredded the *Exit* sign next to the elevator. The EMT fell to the ground, the Uzi flying underneath the row of cars.

"That's two," Kanna said, stepping from behind a pillar. Her ninjato flashed through the air, silently separated the EMT's hands from his wrist. Blood spurted over long-dried oil stains.

The EMT screamed in pain, then passed out from blood loss.

Kanna deposited the ninjato back into a secret fold in her shinobi shōzoku, returned the manriki to her grasp with a simple flick of the wrist. She looked down at the naginata-impaled ninja. "Sabuto. One of the last defectors from Clan Hanasu Nezumi."

"Sabuto?" The guy's eyebrows *did* look familiar. Sabuto tormented the shit out of Nick growing up. Slipped itching powder into his underwear, Visine into his tea.

Made sense he'd gone with Saru.

More sirens wailed in the distance, a different tone from the parade of ambulances that kept pulling up at Turbo City Presbyterian.

Cops.

"Let's go," Kanna said.

They hurried up to the next level, slid into her rental. The inside smelled like bubblegum. When they reached the attendant's kiosk, a few cop cars screeched to a stop in front of the hospital, but the RAV4's bland SUV armor worked like a shinobi shōzoku on the darkest night.

"In plain sight," Kanna said, patting the wheel. "Which way's the airfield?"

Nick looked up and down the boulevard, trying to get his bearings—he'd never needed to go to the hospital before, being in tip-top shape. "Left."

Kanna pulled into traffic. Nick leaned back in his seat, gave himself a once-over. For not having fought or trained in years, he'd acquitted himself pretty well. Granted, some doucher with an Israeli-made machine pistol had almost taken him off the table for good, but he'd bested Sabuto, bane of his childhood.

Old habits die hard. Especially *ninja* habits.

"Take a right here," Nick said. "Jump on the Golan Expressway."

"Got it," Kanna said. She hit the stereo.

"EVERY PERSON DANCE SOON!" the speakers screamed.

Nick tapped along with the beat. Shot Kanna a glance. Her face reddened, she turned away.

This was *their* song.

The world's freshest dance beat soothed Nick's rattled nerves and reminded him that his old life, the one he'd run so far away from, wasn't all bad. Being a ninja had its perks.

Outside, the world kept going—old ladies walking older dogs, hobos walking broken lawnmowers, children raising money to give their parents cancer. Everything seemed offensively normal. Their city was under attack by evil ninjas and these Turbosians barely even noticed.

They got stuck at a light just as the song ended. A couple teenagers holding partially unwrapped burritos came out of a taco joint, drizzling salsa into the exposed innards and trying not to chew the aluminum foil—smiling, laughing, closing their eyes tightly with every bite in sheer ecstasy.

Maybe they didn't care who their mayor was, but they sure as hell cared about fast food. Turbo City didn't need Joe DiFormaggio, but it sure as fuck needed Nick, Rondell, and their crowning baby Fond Dudes.

Kanna pulled onto the expressway.

Up ahead, the blimp hangar loomed large.

TIMES IS TOUGH IN TURBO CITY FOR THE MEGA-CORPORATION OWNER

LAKSHMI RAO PULLED up in front of Turbo Tech headquarters, a sprawling complex of gleaming glass buildings, in her brand-new canary yellow Lambo. Chad Boner rode shotgun, wearing a sick pair of Oakleys and one of those novelty trucker hats with a beer holster stitched to either side, silly straws snaking down to his stubbly jaw. Instead of beer, the holster carried dual cans of Monster energy drink—per Lakshmi, they were on a very important mission, and getting annihilated was a definite no-no. After the bullshit secret council meeting, Lakshmi got all serious-face, told him to keep his wits about him. She'd given him a cursory hand job to tide him over, because she was totally solid like that, then warned him off any further hankity-spankity until they'd saved the city or whatever. Chadwick Junior was a little chafed from their earlier wake 'n bone, so a couple hours reprieve would do him good.

Chad slurped his energy drinks. "What are we doing here again?"

Lakshmi pulled into a spot marked BOSS BITCH and killed the engine. "Like I told you, saving the city."

"But how?"

"With technology. Duh." Lakshmi got out, gently shutting her door.

Chad followed, energy drinks sloshing on either side of his head. Reminded him a bit of the noise machine on the nightstand next to his king-size waterbed back at El Casa Chad, the one with three different settings—ocean noises, whale songs, and Snoop Dogg gently whispering, "Go to beddy-bizzle, for shizzle" over and over again. The thought made him drowsy, so he sucked one of the cans dry.

They walked across the parking lot towards Turbo Tech headquarters. Lakshmi frowned. "It's quiet." She pulled out her phone, called up the Turbo Tech security app. No alerts, but something was off. She opened the live feed for the lobby.

And gasped.

The receptionist's body sprawled across his desk. Bad enough, but his FUCKING HEAD lay nearby in a potted plant, blank gaze canted up at the ceiling cam. Blood covered the walls.

"Dude, so bogus," Chad said.

Lakshmi flicked the image away. Bile bubbled up in her throat. She swallowed, hard, then called security.

The line rang and rang.

Lakshmi glanced back at the Lambo. The smart move was to get out of there in case the killer was still prowling the grounds. No point calling the cops, their hands full with all the ninja nonsense. If Turbo City even *had* a police force anymore.

"Over here," Lakshmi said, pulling Chad behind a bizarre and overly-expensive glass sculpture that somehow managed not to look like anything at all. They ducked down in its shadow while she scrolled through the other camera feeds. The same horrific scene from reception repeated again and again, in seemingly every square inch of the business her father founded back in the 1970s. Hacked-up bodies, slick pools of blood, severed appendages still clutching clipboards and beakers. Stan from Accounting had died with an arrow through his skull and a fire extinguisher in his hands, like a goddamn man. While she didn't see any signs of the attackers, the identities of the perpetrators were obvious.

"Fucking ninjas," Lakshmi said.

"What're we gonna do?" Chad asked, quietly for once.

Lakshmi tossed her phone in her purse, pulled out a yellow plastic gun with bitchin' fins on the side. Instead of a barrel, an antenna curlicued a few inches from the casing and terminated in a ball the size of a marble. "We're going to take back my company, and our city, in that order. Here." She handed him her pepper spray.

"Sweet," Chad said, squinting into the business end. His finger brushed the trigger.

"Careful." Lakshmi wondered what she saw in the idiot, besides his rock-hard abs, prominent jawline, piercing blue eyes, and lofty position in local government. Mostly she figured since she was the smartest person in the greater Turbo City area, there wasn't much point in dating someone who was *almost* as smart as her—might as well go all the way in the other direction.

"I always wanted to get pepper sprayed," Chad said. "That shit looks crazy."

"If we make it through the next couple hours, I'll pepper spray the shit out of you, babe."

Chad lit up. "Really?"

"Yes. Now, come on."

They left the dubious shelter of the abstract glass sculpture and padded across the entryway. In the lobby, Lakshmi tried her best not to look at the beheaded receptionist or feel bad she never bothered to learn his name.

"Dust to dust," Chad said sadly.

Then slurped from his remaining Monster can.

"This way," Lakshmi said, heading for the elevators. Turbo Tech was mostly known for consumer goods—android vacuums, Wifi-enabled thermostats, robot blenders that were just regular blenders with more flashing lights. Unbeknownst to the average citizen, Lakshmi had also procured several contracts with DARPA over the years, developing cutting-edge weapons systems for the military.

That shit went down in Sub Basement C.

Lakshmi raised a hand, let the elevator biometrically scan her. The doors whooshed open. Luckily, nobody had been gruesomely murdered in the elevator. She hit the C button, the doors slid closed once more.

Sweat broke out on her palms. "Be ready for

anything," she said, jitters ravaging her whole body. Because of the DARPA contracts, Sub Basement C was on a separate, closed-circuit security system. If someone hacked her phone, they'd never catch a glimpse of the top-secret shit.

Chad bounced on his heels, gripping the pepper spray. Strangely calm, because despite the blood and gore and his girlfriend's suddenly-serious 'tude, literally everything in his life always worked out super awesome. Chad Boner had never had a bad day, except for once in kindergarten when Timmy Munson made fun of his last name, but then their creepily sex-positive teacher explained to the class that boners were actually a good thing, old men paid pharmaceutical companies thousands of dollars a year to get them, and from then on he'd ruled the shit out of that school.

The elevator stopped. Lakshmi swallowed hard, hoping the doors wouldn't slide open to reveal a, a, whatever the fuck you call a group of ninjas.

The doors opened. Lakshmi tried to aim her ray gun, hands shaking.

She gasped.

All the lights were off.

Quiet as she could, Lakshmi stepped out of the elevator, felt for the light switch.

Flipped it, expecting a swarm of shuriken to rip her to pieces.

The lights came on slowly, gradually illuminating the cavernous laboratory.

Empty.

Of everything that mattered, at least. The ninjas who'd raided her company had, quite obviously, known about Sub Basement C. What she'd been working on, down there in the bowels of the building. What it could do to them. Or *for* them.

Years of work, all gone. And in the hands of men and women who casually slaughtered temp employees whose only purpose in life was to answer phones and play *Minesweeper*.

She sank to her knees, biting back tears. For all intents and purposes, the city *was* Turbo Tech. Her company couldn't exist anywhere else. Just like that, her home, her livelihood, and a bunch of people she considered acquaintances as well as employees were all gone.

"Hey, it's okay," Chad said, sinking down next to her. "See?" He sprayed himself in the face with the pepper spray, collapsed to the ground writhing and gasping for breath, fingernails scraping the metal floor.

"Thanks," Lakshmi said.

That was the real reason she was dating Chad.

He always knew how to cheer her up.

Chad wrenched the final can of Monster free from its holster, poured it directly into his eyes. After a few more minutes of thrashing he finally sat back up, wiping his face with the hem of his cape and breathing heavily. "So," he wheezed, "what are we going to do?"

Lakshmi shrugged. "Stay down here and play strip Monopoly?"

"Huh-huh. Sweet." Chad grinned briefly, then the grin faded. "No, seriously. So those ninjas stole all your shit. What about your *other* shit?"

"Other shit?"

"Yeah, the thing you were telling me about. In Sub Basement D."

Lakshmi sighed. "It's nowhere near ready."

"So? The two of us, working together, we'll get it up and running."

"You're sweet, babe, but I don't think you can help."

Chad pulled off his hat and tossed it away. "I have a master's in electrical engineering and a Ph.D. in nuclear physics."

Lakshmi gaped at him. "What the actual fuck, Chad?"

"What can I say," Chad said, winking and grabbing her ass, "I always liked smart chicks."

MOST RESTAURANTS FAIL WITHIN THE FIRST YEAR

RONDELL HID BEHIND the counter at Fond Dudes, trying not to have a heart attack and wondering what the fuck was going on outside. Having lived in Turbo City his entire life, he'd seen some shit—the East River fire of '94, the smelting factory explosion of '94, the old mayor getting stomped to death by an elephant at the grand opening of Bangalore and More, the World's Biggest South Asian Superstore. Also in '94, come to think of it. Pretty crazy year.

But today was even crazier.

The day had started off all normal and shit. He'd gone to the gym, checked in with his PI to see if she'd snapped any compromising shots of the fucking health inspector—no dice, unfortunately—and then stopped by Fond Dudes to take delivery of an industrial dishwasher (part of him wanted to call up the health inspector on the spot and be like "Look, motherfucker, I *wash* my dishes!" but that would have blown his cover as secret part-owner of the world's first drive-thru fondue joint). The delivery went off without a hitch, and he was about to head over to Crêpes when this guy started banging on the front door. Rondell knew Nick already had quite the following, so he dug a flyer out of his monogrammed satchel and went to tell the guy he was a couple days early.

As soon as he opened the door, the guy fell into the restaurant, babbling incoherently and stumbling all over the place.

Oh shit, Rondell thought, *he's fucking drunk.*

Until he saw the ninja star stuck in the back of the man's head.

The guy collapsed on the floor and fell into convulsions. Rondell knelt next to him, tried to calm him down, but the ninja star had apparently hit something important. Pinkish blood bubbled up from the guy's mouth, he slapped his palms on the tile, and then went still.

Rondell stared at him, unable to believe what he'd witnessed.

But dead bodies don't lie, and neither do ninja stars.

Rondell might've grown up on the mean streets of Turbo City, but he'd also never seen anyone die before except his Grandma Lulu, which is what his parents named the cat. And Grandma Lulu definitely hadn't caught a motherfucking shuriken to the back of her dome piece, she'd fallen asleep and never gotten back up.

Dude on the floor did *not* look like he was sleeping. Nothing peaceful about that motherfucker at all.

Rondell slapped himself a few times until he felt sober enough to stand. Got to his feet, pulled out his phone. Tried to dial 911, but he kept fat-fingering the keypad. Finally remembered he had that robot lady.

"Hey, Shuri, call 911."

"Dialing 911." Shuri sounded like Casey Kasem.

The phone beeped, then he got a busy signal.

"Shit. Shuri, dial 911."

"Dialing 911."

BOMP. BOMP. BOMP.

"Damn." Rondell tried to check the guy's pulse like they do on TV. He couldn't find it, so he held the back of his hand up to the guy's nose—close as he dared, with all that blood.

Nothing.

Rondell tried a few chest compressions, but he didn't expect much. The ninja star was sunk *deep*. He gave up after a couple tries and sank down next to the corpse. What a fucked-up situation. Most restaurants didn't see their first dead body until at least a few hours into opening night, but now they had a stiff days before they'd ever ladle their first cup of fondue. Rondell wasn't a superstitious guy, but that had to be bad luck. Like, really bad luck.

"Oh, shit!"

Something very obvious occurred to Rondell.

Dude had a ninja star stuck in his head. And he'd come from outside.

That very clearly meant there was someone throwing ninja stars nearby. He crept to the door, hazarding a peek. A few crumpled forms lay on the sidewalk. Rondell averted his eyes before he spotted any shuriken.

Pulse still racing, he locked the door and dragged the unfortunate dead man into the back. The walk-in wasn't turned on yet, but it seemed as good a place to put him as any.

Then he grabbed a butcher knife, huddled behind the counter, and tried 911 again for shits and giggles.

BOMP. BOMP. BOMP.

Something crashed across the street. Rondell crept back to the door, knife held awkwardly but firmly in his hand. Someone had driven a semi through the windows of Turbo City Savings & Loan. Black smoke spewed from the engine. After a moment some guy dressed like a sumo wrestler walked out of the truck-hole with a couple gym bags presumably stuffed with cash strung over either shoulder, planted his hands on his hips, and laughed uproariously. A pair of ninjas—*HOLY SHIT, WHAT ARE NINJAS DOING IN TURBO CITY*—followed, wiping off bloody katanas on the pant legs of their ninja outfits, the blood disappearing into the dark fabric.

If Rondell was freaked out before, he was positively apoplectic now.

Especially when the sumo wrestler made eye contact with him.

LAME JOKE ABOUT RUSH HOUR

SARU'S MEN CAUGHT up with Nick and Kanna a mile before the airfield exit.

The blimp hangar was getting closer and closer, and then three ninjas on motorcycles came shooting up behind them, weaving through traffic. Each ninja wore a Pickelhaube helmet and a leather vest over their shinobi shōzoku, the leader swinging a heavy chain over his head like a lasso.

"We've got company," Nick cried. "Punch it!"

Kanna arched an eyebrow. "It's a four-cylinder."

"Is that bad?"

"Great for the planet. Shitty for outracing ninjas."

"Oh." Nick twisted around in his seat. The ninjas were gaining quickly. "Guess we're fighting them."

Kanna tapped the dash. "There's nunchucks in the glove compartment."

Nick's face tightened. "You know I can't."

"Nick—"

"Kanna, I swore an oath. I've broken it today, like a lot. But one thing I won't do, to honor your father—I'm done with nunchucks."

The back window shattered, a shuriken thunked into the dash above the stereo.

Nick plucked the shuriken out, blowing plastic bits onto the floor mats. "Don't worry. I've got this."

One of the ninjas screamed up on their right. Nick rolled down the window, casually flicked the shuriken at the bike.

POP!

The front tire exploded, the forks dropped hard, sparking on the asphalt. The back of the bike bucked up, sending the ninja flying.

"See?" Nick said. "Just drive."

Nick climbed out the window, vaulting atop the RAV4. Wind buffeted him. He sank down on his haunches, finding his balance. Scoped out the scenario. The other two ninjas were coming up on the driver's side. The leader bashed the SUV's side with his chain, smashing another window to bits.

Inside the car, Kanna shook glass out of her hair and tried to keep the car on the road. Horns blared all around them, the other drivers voicing their disapproval at a motherfucking ninja fight breaking out on the freeway.

The RAV4 hit a pothole, Nick wobbled and nearly fell. The other ninja raised a bamboo tube to his mouth.

Pfft!

Time slowed down.

The dart sailed through the air so slowly it might as well have been expectorated through molasses. Nick ducked, the dart sailed over his head and embedded itself in a billboard advertisement for Chez Addis Ababa. The rider took both hands off the handlebars, snatched up another dart from the folds of his shinobi shōzoku, reloaded.

Nick jumped.

Twisted in the air, landed hard on the back of Dart Dude's motorcycle. Before the rider could react he grabbed the ninja's neck and twisted.

SNAP!

Nick pushed the limp body off the bike. It tumbled to the ground, bounced a couple times, got swallowed up by the undercarriage of a trailing tractor-trailer.

The bike pitched wildly. Nick grabbed the handlebars, got it under control. Revved the throttle and zoomed up alongside the leader, who was battering Kanna's door with the chain. She cranked the wheel, trying to knock the motherfucker off his bike, but the guy was clearly an experienced cyclist, zooming out of harm's way and then back into chain-range.

Nick lashed out with a fist, slamming into the leader's helmet. He gritted his teeth at the impact. The leader swung the chain, cracking him across the chest. The bike lurched to the left, swerving into the next lane. Nick twisted his body to avoid a pickup truck's side view mirror, got his bike back under control. The driver of the pickup mashed his brakes, a sedan slammed into his tailgate.

The terrible sound of rending metal filled the air.

Nick glanced right. The leader had his chain wrapped around Kanna's neck, pulling her halfway out the window. She slid one hand between the chain and her neck-flesh, kept the other on the wheel. The RAV4 veered all over the highway. Cars and trucks screeched to a halt on either side, eager to stay the fuck away from whatever this bullshit was.

The leader yanked his chain, pulling Kanna along with him. She lost her grip on the wheel, both hands grabbing the chain.

The exit for the airfield disappeared behind them.

Nick didn't know what to do—if he'd only taken the nunchucks, he could have easily broken the ninja's arms, letting Kanna slide free. But now, if he knocked the ninja off his bike Kanna might well come with him, snapping her neck in the process.

One thing Nick could not abide.

Nick popped up onto the bike seat, daredevil-style, and jumped.

Praying he got the trajectory right, he sailed through the air in an eons-long fall—

That thankfully fucking ended in a hard-ass bellyflop on the roof of the RAV4.

His commandeered motorcycle, riderless, kept on for a second and then laid itself down. Kanna still struggled with the chain. The semi-driverless RAV4 bucked underneath him, threatening to throw him off.

Up ahead, a cluster of yellow signs told him they were about to enter a construction zone.

Down in the SUV, Kanna was kind of driving with her feet. She couldn't even snatch up a weapon, since she needed both hands to keep that asshole from yanking her out the window.

Nick slipped a hand inside the broken driver's window, shallowly slashing his wrist on glass shards, gripping the frame tight. With his free hand, he reached down and grabbed the chain in the middle, jerking it as hard as he could.

The ninja flew off his bike, slammed into Kanna's door, dropping his end of the chain.

Then he hit the road.

Hard.

Nick dropped back down into the passenger's seat. Kanna was back at the wheel, the chain gone, rubbing her throat, wicked red marks between her fingers.

She swallowed. "Ow, can't believe that asshole—"

Oh hey, remember that road work up ahead?

LET'S CHECK IN WITH OUR DISAPPROVING OUT-OF-WORK EDITOR

SOMEWHERE OUTSIDE Nick's apartment, a scraggly man stumbled up to the newspaper kiosk and leaned down to inspect the afternoon addition with bloodshot eyes.

"Masked . . . Miscreants . . . Make . . . off . . . with . . . Mayor!" he mumbled, then reared back and kicked the kiosk, leaving only a scuff mark. The man hopped a couple times on one foot, then regained his balance/composure and trudged away, shoulders slumped, mumbling to himself over and over again.

"Goddamn alliteration."

CONVALESCENCE

SHAME.
'The vile feeling permeated every cell of Skip Baxter's body. He hadn't felt like this in a long time. Pain, sure—even sparring with five-year-olds he got his ass kicked on a regular basis. But no matter how many times a three-foot-tall pixie with a strawberry blonde ponytail knocked him to the mat, he got back up, dusted himself off, and told her in no uncertain terms he'd *let* her do that. And in a strange way, he was proud, knowing he'd taught her the roundhouse that swept his flabby legs out from under him.

But now he'd been knocked to the mat by a guy who *sounded* like a five-year-old girl, permanently.

Hawk Dragon Martial Arts was fucking over, man.

Ironically, the dojo started because of a night he'd felt much like this. Years ago, before Marsha and his dojo, he'd been a different man, a drunken, Binoca-breathed playboy without a care in the world. Back then, Skip was the Most Dangerous Cad in Turbo City. He must have made it with three or four women over the span of seventeen years. One even let him do butt stuff.

The night in question, he spotted a gorgeous blonde sipping a martini across the bar, a pale line around her ring finger and a faraway look in her eyes. Skip sidled over, kept on walking to the bathroom. Splashed water in his face, told himself he'd pull up a stool and say hello if she was still alone. Walked back out, saw she was, decided to play some *Golden Tee* and if he got a hole-in-one, *then* he'd go talk to her.

He'd hit six by the time he ran out of quarters.

Skip counted his cash. Enough for two drinks. Told himself he'd count to ten and go over. Then twenty.

Then five hundred.

Then the bartender called last call and she was gone anyway.

"Shit," Skip muttered. "I was about to make my move."

On the way home, a homeless guy in a wheelchair mugged him.

Skip woke up the next day, looked in the mirror, and fucking hated what he saw. He vowed to transform himself into a total badass, the kind of guy you'd never dream of mugging without at least one working leg. He tried to do a push-up, didn't much care for it, and settled in on the couch to watch old martial arts movies instead.

Three days later, he'd mastered karate and opened Hawk Dragon with a generous loan from Aunt Lindy, the famous racecar driver. Like that, the worst moment of his life became the proudest moment of his life.

He was a sensei, a badass, the Most Dangerous Man in Turbo City, equipped by Mother Nature herself with two incredibly Deadly Weapons™.

What was he now? A pincushion? A cripple? Fated

to wither away in a hospital bed until his bedsores got infected and he died from sepsis?

Fuck.

That.

"Ca-caw," Skip whispered. "Fwoosh."

Skip rang for the nurse.

Ten minutes later, she stuck her head in. "I'm not giving you a handjob. Couldn't reach it if I wanted to with your cast."

"No handjobs. Get me an electric wheelchair. And a gun."

"We don't have guns."

"Just the wheelchair, then."

The nurse shrugged. "Okay. Ordinarily we wouldn't let a patient in your condition leave the hospital, but you're kind of a piece of shit."

"Thank you."

The nurse left.

Skip Baxter, the Most Crippled Man in Turbo City, stared up at the ceiling and thought about how, precisely, he was about to unfuck that.

He tried to smile and passed out again.

DECONSTRUCTION ZONE

KANNA PLOWED INTO the back of a cement mixer.

The impact threw Nick forward into the dash, cracking him a good one, then bounced him back into his seat. Smoke poured into the car.

Everything looked strange and shimmery, blurred out of focus. He blinked until the curved edges of the world sharpened again. He felt his head, found a bloody knot.

A zig-zagging crack split the dash, like a stump struck by lightning. Beyond the windshield, the ass-end of the cement mixer filled Nick's vision.

"You okay?" Kanna mumbled.

"Think so—"

Yeah, NOPE.

The chute from the cement mixer was sticking through a large hole in the windshield, terminating above the center console. A couple inches to either side and Nick or Kanna would've been skewered.

Even over the ringing in his ears, Nick could hear it. Or feel it, rather.

The vibrations from the slowly-turning cement cylinder.

Either they had the worst timing in the world,

rear-ending a piece of construction equipment during the union-mandated seventeen minutes a day when the road crew was actually working, or—

Sludgy, chunky concrete shot out of the chute.

Nick recoiled, slamming into the door. He groped for the handle. Kanna did the same.

The cement disgorged quicker than Nick expected, shooting all over the console, spewing into the backseat. Even with the shattered back windows acting as a release valve, the SUV would soon be filled from carpet to domelight.

Nick pushed open the door, falling in wet cement. He got back to his feet, turned—

And caught a fucking SHOVEL TO THE FACE, SON.

The impact threw him back against the RAV4. He got his hands up in time to block the next strike, knocking the shovel away.

His attacker, a construction crew member in an orange vest and yellow hardhat with a ninja mask, swung the shovel again. Nick ducked, shot in and tackled the guy.

"Ayyy!" someone yelled, landing a kick to Nick's ribs.

Nick winced, rolled, popping back up to his feet. Another ninja construction worker helped the first attacker up, this new assailant rocking a sledgehammer.

Nick wasn't surprised— shinobi shōzoku looked badass, but were rarely worn when actually doing ninja shit. The OG ninjas dressed like field hands, monks, servants, anything to blend in amongst the population. Most ninja weapons, from nunchucks to kusarigama, began life as farming implements. So two ninjas wearing orange vests and hard hats, toting construction tools?

All part of a grand tradition.

A scuffle broke out on the other side of the car, lots of thumps and thwacks and *oh dear gods*. Kanna would have to take care of herself—something she was quite capable of.

Nick wasn't sure he could say the same.

Sledgehammer-Man swung. Nick dodged, the hammer chunking a heavy dent in the car's back panel.

Shovel wielded his own weapon like a poleaxe, jabbing Nick in the stomach with the tip, narrowly missing his solar plexus.

Nick kicked Shovel under the jaw. Shovel's head snapped back. Nick jumped when Sledgehammer swung at his knees. Landed, threw a straight left at Sledgehammer's face.

Bone crunched, blood sprayed from the dude's broken nose.

Nick clipped him with a quick one-two combo, followed by a roundhouse to the side of the guy's head. Sledgehammer dropped his weapon, staggering back.

Rolling through wet concrete, Nick snatched up the sledgehammer and spun around to block Shovel's latest attack. He bashed the hammer into Shovel's chest. The man stumbled through the wet concrete, falling on his o-ring. Nick whirled, swinging the hammer up and over his head, smashing it down into Sledgehammer's knee.

CRUNCH!

The ninja screamed, drew his shattered knee into his chest. Out of the fight. Nick turned back to finish off Shovel—back on his feet, spinning the spade like a bo staff. The shovelhead slashed through the air.

Nick blocked the attack with the sledgehammer's shaft, which broke in two. He tossed the wooden end, ducked another spade swing, and jumped, ricocheting off the RAV4 and spinning back at Shovel.

He brought the foreshortened hammer down on Shovel's head.

SHUNK!

The blow crushed Shovel's skull. Nick landed back on the shoulder, still clutching the hammer. The empty-eyed attacker swayed and fell face down in the concrete. Cement splatted on Nick's boots.

He swiveled around in a circle to look for more attackers, breathing heavily. Over on Kanna's side of the car, a hardy commotion was still going on, but Nick couldn't see a thing though the cement-filled RAV4.

Nick was about to dive across the hood to join Kanna when a fierce pain erupted in his thigh.

"Die!" The broke-kneed ninja wrenched a stiletto from Nick's leg, blood spurting out and splashing his yellow helmet, tried to jab him again but Nick danced back, the stiletto sunk into the berm. Before the ninja could yank it out, Nick busted his asshole ninja hand with the hammer. Again, the man yelped in pain, clutching an obliterated body part.

Nick whacked him with the hammer until both his helmet and the ninja skull beneath were nothing but jagged, shattered fragments. He sucked in a few harsh breaths, chest heaving, covered in blood and brains and wet cement, forearms burning.

Something burned beyond the RAV4. Thick black smoke roiled skyward. Nick ripped off his belt and tied it around his leg to staunch the bleeding, then dashed around the car.

A pile of orange-vested bodies lay in the wet cement. A flatbed truck parked fifteen or twenty feet away burned with abandon, stinking up the air with molten metal and flaming transmission fluid.

Beyond the flatbed, Kanna faced off against another ninja, this one driving a backhoe. He swung the boom at her like a scorpion flicking its tail. Kanna easily dodged, the bucket scoring empty air, and unleashed the manriki. With one smooth motion she pulled him from the cab, he fell to the ground at her feet.

The ninjato flashed, piercing the man's heart.

"That all of them?" Nick yelled.

In response, four more ninjas vaulted over the concrete-filled RAV4 and surrounded Nick, wielding a variety of ninja weapons.

The broken hammer in his hand felt sadly inadequate.

Kanna rushed towards him, but a van screeched to a halt on the other side of the freeway. More ninjas jumped out, streaming across the median, unleashing a hurricane of shuriken. Kanna flipped out of the way, then Nick lost her behind the truck.

His own ninjas circled him.

Nick moved in a smaller, tighter circle, feinting with the hammer.

The ninjas mirrored him, swiping and stabbing.

Once, Nick would have wiped the floor with them. Now?

"Hai!" shouted one ninja.

The others converged, pressing in and swinging weapons. A cudgel-wielding ninja knocked the hammer from his hands. Nick fought back, lashing out with wild punches and kicks, rolling between ninjas. He fought to break free of the circle—if he could get to Kanna, they could watch each other's backs, use wheel techniques to nerf the ninjas' numerical advantage.

An errant ninjato peeled a chunk of flesh off Nick's shoulder. He barely felt it, leaping up into a flying kick that sent the swordsman flying.

Nick landed, two more ninjas immediately attacking with kanabō—wickedly-spiked metal clubs. One swung low, the other high. Nick flipped backwards, hand-springing into a second flip over the head of yet another ninja holding a yari—a long spear.

He hit the ground, still too close. Smoke from the burning truck stung his eyes, choked his lungs, lent the whole scene a strange, dream-like texture.

The yari-wielder whirled, using her extra-long reach to leave a cruel slice across Nick's chest. When she whipped the spear around again, Nick held his position until the last possible second, the blade missing his ear by millimeters, and grabbed the shaft. He wrenched it out of the ninja's hand and dropped back again, spinning the shaft around and sweeping her legs out from under her.

WHUMPH!

The kanabō guys leapt over the fallen spearholder. Nick thrust the yari straight through the one on the left's leg, the blade sailing through his thigh and out the other side.

Stuck through his leg, the ninja wavered and dropped to his good knee, losing his kanabō in the process.

Nick dove forward, grabbed the dropped cudgel and crushed the other kanabō-wielder's skull.

The former yari-holder sprung at Nick, kicking him in the chest. He fell backwards, losing the club. The swordsman pounced from behind, slicing the air.

Nick twisted sideways, caught the flat of the blade between his palms. They strained, Nick and the ninja, the attacker trying mightily to force the sword down—

Nick shoved the sword aside, threw a shoulder into the man. He stumbled back a step, Nick bombarded him with punches, the impacts staggering the man further.

The yari-wielder jumped on his back, sliding a forearm under his throat. Nick gulped and hinged at the waist, pitching her forward. She landed on top of the burning truck's engine.

Flames licked at her body, she screamed.

Nick gave the final, still-standing ninja a quick combo, jabs and a heavy right knocking him to the ground.

Then ended the ninja with his own ninjato.

"Yah!" someone behind him cried.

Nick spun, ninjato at the ready. The yari-wielder was running at him.

Still on fire.

Ducking a flaming roundhouse kick, Nick swung the ninjato, the blade sailing straight through her neck and sending her head flipping end-over-end to land in the flaming, blackened outline of what used to be a flatbed.

Nick stumbled away from the truck in search of clean air. A breath, that's all he needed—

The sky went black.

Or so it seemed, before he felt the net enmeshing him. Blows crashed into his back, his shoulders, his head. He tried to turtle up, but the net clung to his limbs. Seemed like there were hundreds of them, thousands, all gathered around and kicking the shit out of him while burning oil choked his lungs and heavy machinery hissed and crackled.

Something grabbed his ankle, then he was skidding out of the net on his stomach. Kanna stood over him holding her manriki. A flick of the wrist unwrapped the chain from his ankle. One hand darted into her shinobi shōzoku, then silver shuriken flashed.

Shuk, shuk, shuk!

"Come on," Kanna said, holding out a hand.

Nick grabbed her forearm, let her help him to his feet. He glanced over his shoulder, saw three ninjas with shuriken stuck in their eyes and throats, tangled in their own net. "Thanks."

"Don't mention it. Come on, we have to get out of here."

Another van screeched up out of the smoke, side door swinging open.

The inside bristled with assault rifles.

"Nick, go!" Kanna screamed.

They both wheeled, rushing for the cement-filled RAV4. Bullets whizzed past, peppering the side of the SUV, kicking up dirt, crashing into dead ninjas. Kanna jumped over the SUV, Nick following, a bullet whizzing by his ear.

Dropping down on the other side of the RAV4,

Kanna pointed at the brick wall, twenty feet away. Automatic gunfire ripped through the air, shredding the car. "There, maybe we can lose them."

Nick nodded.

Together, they broke for the wall, arms and legs pumping furiously. More bullets stippled the barrier, poofs of concrete dust rising in the air.

Kanna reached the wall first, bounded over. She popped up over the top of the wall, motioning wildly. "Nick, come on!"

A bullet zapped by her head, she ducked back down.

More bullets stitched the ground behind Nick. He reached the wall, jumped and cleared it, flipping over the cement barrier, but caught the toe of his shoe on the top of the wall. Off-balance, he hit the ground hard, whacking his shoulder out of joint.

"Argh," Nick said, clutching his shoulder. He willed the pain away, staggered to his feet, the arm hanging limply at his side.

More bullets whacked into the wall behind them. Nick scanned their surroundings. They'd ended up in a neighborhood, a nice-looking one, green lawns and tire swings. A blonde kid rode his Big Wheel down the sidewalk.

"Uh oh. Where should we—"

"I don't know, too many civilians."

Nick spotted it. Across the street, below the curb. "Storm drain."

"Sweet."

They ran for the drain. Men yelled behind them, somebody crested the wall and jumped down. An AK yapped at them.

As one, like fucking Olympic divers, Nick and Kanna bent forward and dove into the storm drain.

RONDELL VS. SLAG

THE LAUGHING SUMO WRESTLER handed off his bags to a ninja on either side of him and strode across the street, belly jiggling with menace.

Rondell yelped and backed away from the door, slipping on the bloodstain the dead guy left behind. The knife went flying. He landed hard on his ass. He crab-crawled backwards, bumping up against the counter.

The sumo crossed the street quickly, slapping one meaty fist into an open palm. Something was strapped to his waist. Rondell squinted at the object, panicked mind figuring maybe if he could make sense of that, he could make sense of everything, the sort of desperate magical thinking unique to the utterly goddamn doomed.

Run, dumbass, Rondell thought, pulling himself to his feet. He couldn't remember the last time he took a breath.

The sumo walked straight through the front door.

No hesitation, one moment he was standing in front of the door, the next he was walking *through* it in a spray of shattered glass, ripping the metal frame off the hinges. It crashed to the floor. Tiny cuts nicked his shoulders, his belly, his forehead, but his expression never changed.

A big fucking gaptoothed smile.

The sumo paused inside the restaurant, looked at his handiwork. "Made a real dog's breakfast of your entryway, mate. 'Pologies. She'll be all right, you get a good contractor on 'er." His bloody forehead crinkled. "What's this place?"

Rondell swallowed, mouth dry. "Restaurant."

The sumo slapped his stomach, the motion rippling all the way to his saggy lats. "I know, what *kind?*"

"Fondue."

"Ah, a fondy! Haven't seen one 'a these in ages." The sumo scanned the restaurant, eyes settling on the logo. "What's that, then?"

Rondell cast an uneasy glance at the logo. "It's, uh, the name of the place. I didn't make it up."

"Huh. *Fond Dudes*. And what's that, two guys hugging? You some kinda poofter?"

"Uh—"

"Don't matter none. Hell, I used to hug other men in nappies all the livery-longadoo, who am I to talk? Say, all this carrying on's giving me a bugger of an appetite. I'll take five of whatever you got. Name's Slag, by the way."

Rondell cast an uneasy glance at the kitchen, the empty refrigerator, the lonely, unmated gas hookups for the stove that wasn't going to be delivered until Monday. "I'd love to, but we aren't open yet."

"Tell me you've at least got a coldie? That's a beer-o, for you Yanks."

"Not—" Rondell caught himself. Despite the guy's

overly friendly demeanor, he'd just walked through a plate glass door, robbed a bank, and was probably at least tangentially responsible for the poor dead guy jinxing up the walk-in with his fucking dead guy mojo. Rondell couldn't exactly picture him saying *All righty then* if he explained they didn't even serve beer. "Not out here," Rondell continued. "In the back. I'll get you one."

Slag grinned. "Dandy-o!"

Rondell quickly headed into the back, trying to come up with a plan. He could head out the emergency exit, but his car was out front. He'd need to circle around, but he could make it. The guy was fast, but—

Slag started whistling a tune Rondell didn't recognize, but it might as well have been the *Jeopardy!* theme. The message was clear.

Rondell's time was running out.

He approached the empty fridge, wishing Nick were there. Goofy as his business partner was, the two of them might have a snowball's chance in hell against the massive, absurdly cheerful man in the lobby. Alone, Rondell's only chance was to run—

Somebody screamed out in the alley, the sound abruptly cutting off.

Well, shit.

Rondell wasn't going out there.

"'Ay! How 'bout that coldie?"

"Coming!"

Rondell glanced at the walk-in. Hiding out with a dead guy was preferable to whatever Slag would do when he found out Rondell didn't have a fucking coldie, and the walk-in was built like a fortress. Too bad it didn't lock from the inside.

Hands shaking, he opened the fridge, hoping like hell one of the contractors left a Bud behind.

Nothing, not even a box of baking soda. He'd take his chances outside—

Out of the corner of his eye, Rondell spotted the gas hookups. Shot a quick glance at the walk-in, back at the gas.

The idea was just crazy enough to work.

"Uh, main cooler's empty, gonna check down below!" Rondell yelled over his shoulder, dropping to a crouch.

"You're acting a mite sheepy there, mate."

"Nope, it's, everything's new. Don't know where stuff—" He cranked the handles on the jets as far as they would go, "—is."

Rondell reached for his Zippo, figuring he'd dart into the walk-in and toss the lighter back out after him. And then pray like a motherfucker.

He rose, braced to run—

Slag stood between him and the door.

"What's this, then?" Slag said, pointing at the silently whooshing gas jets. "You going all Al Qaedy on me, blowin' up yer customers? Kinda rude, you ask me."

Rondell ran.

Not towards the walk in, towards the non-existent front door.

He managed three steps before Slag grabbed his collar, yanking him back.

Rondell dangled in the air, shoes suspended three feet off the ground, looking down into Slag's face. The guy stank like moldy cheese.

"I'm sorry, okay? I thought you were going to kill me."

"Well, I am now!"

Rondell gulped.

"Just kidding," Slag said, lowering Rondell until they were eye level, Rondell's shoe tips brushing the floor. "I was always gonna kill ya."

"Wait—"

Rondell spun, or the world spun, the barely-finished interior of Fond Dudes careening by in a whirling kaleidoscope and then he was weightless. All too briefly—he slammed into the wall, slid down the freshly-painted logo, crumpled into a heap on the floor, semi-conscious.

The massive shadow looming over him snapped him back to reality.

Rondell tried to back up, but there was nowhere to go.

Slag towered over him, hands on his hips. "Hurts, yeah? That's for starters. I'm gonna break every bonearoo in yer worthless body." Slag reached down—

Rondell growled and lashed out with a foot, nailing the sumo in the junk.

Slag looked down at his crotch, back at Rondell. "That all ya got? I been zonked in me dilly-doggle by the best dick-kickers in the world. You're not fit to carry their nappies. Here, have a proper go."

Rondell kicked him again.

"Ha! Almost tickled, it did. I'll give ya one more free shot. How's that?"

The smell of gas was overwhelming. Rondell fingered his Zippo—if he was dead anyway, why the fuck not? At least he could take this asshole with him, and maybe someday Nick would build a new restaurant overtop the smoking crater where the original Fond Dudes had been, put up a statue of him or some shit. Maybe with a plaque. Rondell always wanted his name on a plaque.

"Saving your strength, eh? Well hurry, I don't got all day to stand here waiting for a kick in the old janky dangle."

Rondell cocked back his foot, ready for one last, incredibly desperate attempt at saving his ass via the most epic dick-kick the human penis had ever seen.

That's when he finally realized what the weird-ass bulge on the dude's side was.

Colostomy bag!

Rondell snatched the bag away with a wet ripping sound. A round incision the size of a silver dollar made of poop winked back at him.

Slag grunted and stumbled back a few ponderous steps. "Hey! What the—"

Trying not to think about what he was holding, Rondell lunged and slapped the poop bag in Slag's face.

SPLUCH!

Slag cried out, hands batting at the shit bag clinging to his face like Xenomorph larvae. He stumbled backwards into the refrigerator, stainless steel doors accordioning inward. Slag dropped to his knees, coughing and puking and swearing vigorously in what Rondell assumed was Australian.

"Ech! Ya shoved a poopery-doo right in me laughing gear! What kinda—Christchurch, I was only gonna kill ya, no—HURK—call for it, no—HURK HURK HURK!"

Rondell realized he was standing there like an

asshole, watching a five-hundred-pound man puke his own shit onto the floor, and all of a sudden it was goddamn Junior Prom all over again.

Except this time *he* was in control.

Rondell sprinted for the walk-in, vaulted the vomitous sumo and somehow landed on his feet. He got a hand on the walk-in and yanked it open. He ducked inside, pulling the Zippo from his pocket.

Slag clambered to his feet, the empty colostomy bag on the floor, shit and puke smeared across his ruddy face. "What the fuckery-doo, mate?" The incision in his side quivered, then a turd slid out, falling to the floor with a loud *splat*.

Rondell swallowed back his own rising gorge, grabbed the interior door handle with one hand and flicked his Zippo with the other.

One of Slag's eyes went wide with terror. The other was presumably too filled with poo. He raised his hands, placating. "Now now, I think we might've—"

"G'DAY, MOTHAFUCKA!" Rondell tossed the lighter, slammed the door shut and dove to the floor, pulling the dead guy's body atop him and then—

KA.

FUCKING.

BOOM.

SOME ASSHOLE EATS ETHIOPIAN FOOD

KUNDARAI SARU LOOKED out over the city. Soon to be *his* city. In less than an hour, he'd beat the shit out of the sniveling, piss-drenched mayor and assume his mantle.

After that, nothing could stop him.

Leading an evil ninja clan had its perks, but what he really wanted was total worldwide domination. With Turbo City under his thumb, he'd gain a serious foothold in the U.S., from which he could launch attacks on all the other major metropolitan areas. Los Angeles. New York. Wheeling, West Virginia. There'd be resistance, of course. The governor was undoubtedly calling in the National Guard. But once he was declared mayor, the optics of sending in the troops would be unpalatable. The Americans loved their precious democracy, and their even-more-precious loopholes. And if they did question the legitimacy of his office, his ninjas were busy fortifying the city and recruiting more troops.

Plus, he'd seized Turbo Tech and the highly-advanced weapons systems Lakshmi Rao so kindly developed for him. Sasayaku had checked in an hour before, informing him of her mission's success. She'd already secured the package and returned to base, and now she was presumably trolling the city for Kanna Kikuchi. Daisuke confirmed the Turbo City police brass no longer existed, and Slag was undoubtedly sowing chaos and destruction on every street corner.

Everything was going according to—

BZZZZT. "Master?"

Saru turned away from the city and pulled out his walkie-talkie. "Yes, Daisuke?"

"We've got a problem."

Of course we fucking do. "Yes?"

"Slag hasn't checked in."

"That's all? He's probably looting a Honey Baked Ham."

The door opened and a ninja trainee entered carrying a platter of kik alicha. The heady scent of peas stewed in turmeric filled the room, his stomach growled. He motioned for the trainee to set the plate down on his desk.

"His men said they haven't seen him since the bank job. He headed across the street, for what they couldn't say, and then there was an explosion."

"Good. That was his job. Explosions and the like."

"I know, but—"

"Forget Slag. Ready the camera."

"Hai!" Daisuke clicked off.

Saru ambled over to the table, inhaling the rich scent of Ethiopian cuisine, and settled into his chair.

No way was he becoming mayor of Turbo City on an empty stomach.

AN UNSUBTLE HOMAGE TO PETER LAIRD AND KEVIN EASTMAN

THE SEWER WAS dark and smelled like shit. But Nick and Kanna were ninjas so the whole dark thing was cool, and they didn't smell so awesome themselves, what with all the bloodletting, front-and-back-flipping, car surfing, motorcycle neck snapping, near concrete drowning, and all the other goddamn nonsense they'd been through over the last however the fuck long it was.

"They missed your femoral artery," Kanna said, inspecting the wound in Nick's leg. Dark blood clotted near the small, neat puncture in his thigh. She gave his other wounds a once-over. All of the fleshy variety.

Except the shoulder.

Adrenaline got him into the sewer, but if some subterranean ninjas jumped them, he wouldn't be able to put up much of a fight.

Kanna placed her hands on his shoulder. "Count to ten."

"Okay. One."

Kanna snapped his shoulder back into place.

Nick screamed, spasmed and smacked his head against the concrete pylon. Sucked in a breath, then got up, rotated the arm, threw a few punches at the air. "Feels like new!"

Kanna smiled. "Ninja magic."

"Thanks," Nick replied, giving her a slight hug—awkward, and all too brief.

"Come on," Kanna said, turning away. "Let's go find this stupid airfield."

They wandered through the sewers, their passage lit only by small flashlights Kanna helpfully pulled from her shinobi shōzoku. Rats skittered in the shadows, every corridor looked much like the last. There wasn't much room to walk on the concrete pylons, they had to stay stooped and move in a near-crouch, but it was better than slopping through the totally shitty water.

"Are you sure we're headed to the airfield?" Nick asked, voice echoing off the cement.

Kanna glanced at the passageways yawning off into deeper darkness. "Not really. We need to find a manhole or something."

Nick checked his watch. "It's 4:15."

"I know. We'll get there."

"We have to. If Saru becomes mayor, I'm finished."

Kanna chuckled lightly. "We all are."

"Why's he doing this, anyway?"

Kanna's shoe scraped the concrete, she paused to get her balance. "Same reason assholes do anything. Power."

They kept moving. Nick fought the urge to check his watch. He didn't want to know how many precious minutes they were bleeding, lost in the sewer. He wondered what Rondell was up to, if he was okay. Even though Rondell could handle himself, Nick couldn't help but worry. What if he saved the mayor, got him to sign the license still neatly-folded in his bloody, cement-spattered jeans and—

"Nick?" Kanna waited for him to look at her. "Back there, those assholes almost killed us."

"Ninjas'll do that."

"Yeah, but . . . " Kanna trailed off, turned her face away.

Nick stopped, but a hand on her shoulder. "What?"

She shrugged his hand away. "That guy with the chain, when he was choking me—Nick, why won't you use nunchucks?"

"You know why."

"No, I don't fucking know why!" Kanna shoved him, backing Nick into the sloping tunnel wall. "You can't keep going around bare-handed. You're so much better with nunchucks. Worlds better, nobody can touch you. And yet for whatever fucking reason, you'd rather just, just tie your hands behind your back, and hope for the best. Why, Nick?"

Nick looked away, off into the darkness.

Into the past.

OBLIGATORY NESTED FLASHBACK

IN THE MIDDLE of the night, the master called to him.

The boy rose from his pallet and moved silently through the compound, home to Clan Hanasu Nezumi. No lights brightened the interior, but he could walk the halls blindfolded and easily find his way. After all, he'd lived there for many years, ever since the accident killed his parents. Master Kikuchi, his mother's uncle, took him in, made him everything he was. Or tried—the boy was recalcitrant, always sneaking into the kitchen to pester the cooks instead of focusing on his ninja lessons. Then, on the day of his thirteen birthday, Master Kikuchi sat him down and explained his destiny. The great kitsune Mr. Shifty Whiskers Ph.D. came to the master in a vision, revealed that the boy, humble though he was, carried the power of the clan's founder Orenji-iro no Kame in his heart. No mere orphan, after all.

He was the Chosen One™.

Though the boy harbored no desire to become a ninja, let alone THE ninja, he had no choice. Master

Kikuchi raised him like his own. Cared for him. Loved him.

How could he let him down?

After that day, Nick trained harder. Part of him would have still preferred to watch the cooks, to learn their secrets—such art offered far more intrigue than ninjutsu, which came easily to him and required little effort.

He stifled such desires, threw himself into his lessons.

Over the next few years, his skills grew. Nick and Kanna pushed each other, jockeying back and forth for the top spot in their class, and finally served as co-valedictorians when they all graduated from ninja school. Nick's path seemed set in stone.

On his eighteenth birthday, Kikuchi finally decided Nick was ready to master the most dangerous weapon ever invented.

Nunchaku.

"The nunchuck," Master Kikuchi explained, "began as a simple farming tool, like most of our weapons. Easily concealed, devastating in battle. Quickly, though, it fell out of favor, for the nunchuck proved as deadly to the wielder as to their enemies. Many dashed their own brains out. All agreed the nunchaku held a hidden power, but none dared seek it out.

"Until," and then Master Kikuchi ran a loving hand over the wooden turtle totem he wore on a leather thong around his neck, "came Orenji-iro no Kame. His technique, Kame-do, proved unstoppable. The shoguns sent legions of samurai against him, killing his brothers, but in the end Orenji-iro prevailed. Melted down the swords of his enemies and, from a lightning-struck tree, forged the ultimate weapon.

"The Sticks of Heaven."

Even young Nick, reluctant ninja though he was, knew enough to *ooh* and *ahh* appropriately at this part of the story.

"For a thousand years, no one has proven worthy to wield the nunchaku of Orenji-iro no Kame. But you, Nick of Clan Hanasu Nezumi—the Sticks are your destiny."

"Me?"

"But first, you must master nunchaku. Here." Kikuchi handed Nick a pair of foam tubes held together with string.

Nick looked doubtfully at the prop weapon. For years they'd let him train with razor-sharp katana, ninjato, sai.

He felt like he'd been busted down to white belt.

Kikuchi must have seen the look in his eyes, for he placed a strong hand on Nick's shoulder and said, "Buck up, buttercup."

Nick did.

The other students snickered behind his back at the sight of the so-called "Chosen One" *JERKOFF MOTIONS* twirling a fake weapon. All but Kanna. On those long, endless nights when Nick stayed up in the courtyard, bashing himself in the forehead again and again with the fauxchucks, she was right there with him, manriki in hand.

Sometimes Nick sensed Kikuchi watching them from behind a shoji, but when he turned there was no one there.

Once he could go all night without bopping himself, Master Kikuchi let him graduate to real nunchaku. He sensed the immense power inherent in the weapons immediately. His first sessions were slow, tentative, but he soon found he could spin the nunchucks faster than a jet engine and dash a practice dummy to splinters in a single strike.

"Such power," Kikuchi said simply, on one of the rare occasions when he explicitly observed Nick's training.

While before ninjutsu was an obligation, with nunchucks in hand Nick actually felt thrilled by what he was doing. He forgot about the mysteries of the kitchen, focusing exclusively on learning the secrets of the chain-bound sticks. The master was happy, sure.

But Nick was, too.

Then *that* night.

Master Kikuchi called to him in his sleep. Nick immediately awakened. He made his way across the compound to the master's chambers. No one was about, except for a new student, the older man named Kundarai Saru, who was watching a football game on the satellite. Nick said a brief hello and proceeded to Kikuchi's room, where torches still burned and the master himself waited, legs crossed primly beneath him.

"My son," Kikuchi said, "It is time."

"Time?"

"Yes. For this!" Kikuchi pointed to two sets of nunchaku on the floor. They were simple, unadorned, the wood black as obsidian, the aged chains gleaming like the day they'd been forged.

Nick waited, unsure what to do.

Kikuchi motioned to the nunchaku. "Now, Nick, take up the Sticks of Heaven. Seize your destiny!"

Nick crossed the room slowly, reverently, heart pounding. He picked up the Sticks, a crackle of energy running up his hands, his forearms, the tingle filling his entire body.

They felt good. Right.

Kikuchi laughed. "Don't just stand there. Show me what you've got!"

"Hai!"

Nick twirled the Sticks, power flowing through his body, demonstrating all the forms he'd practiced over the years. He felt unbearably close to something more powerful than he could imagine. The Sticks sparkled, warm in his hands, lightning sizzling with every swing, every snap, every—

The nunchucks flew from his hands and cracked Kikuchi square in the forehead.

The master's head snapped back, his body crumpled to the ground.

Nick ran to him. He dropped to his knees. A red welt bloomed between the older man's eyes, which lay shut with finality.

"Master? Master!" Nick shook him, felt for a pulse.

Nothing.

Nick turned his head and puked on the floor of the master's quarters.

What had he done? What the ACTUAL FUCK had he done?

Nick checked Kikuchi one more time, saw no signs of life. He staggered to his feet, panicked.

Turned.

And ran.

THINGS THAT SHOULD HAVE BEEN BROUGHT TO MY ATTENTION YESTERDAY

KANNA GAPED AT HIM. *"That's* why you ran away?"

Nick hung his head. He'd never told a single soul what happened that night, not even Pierre (who'd often looked at him knowingly and said, "Vous avez une obscurité dans votre cœur, mon ami," but never pushed further). For years he'd imagined this moment, thinking if he could only admit to Kanna what happened, maybe she'd hate him, but at least he'd feel better.

He didn't.

If anything, he felt worse. Much worse. Kind of like getting kicked in the dick, but instead of the dick it was his heart.

Kanna's hands flew to her face, for a moment Nick thought she might be overcome with grief, or righteous anger, but then she snorted, once.

"What?"

And then she was laughing, doubled over, tears streaming down her cheeks. She braced herself on her knees, head bobbing up and down, her mirth echoing up and down the tunnels.

Nick frowned. He'd been prepared for a torrent of abuse, maybe even a furious ninja attack—one he wouldn't have resisted—but laughter? He'd known Kanna all his life, she'd never gone in for cruel mockery, even when Tub-Tub split his shinobi shōzoku down the middle climbing a wall or when Haruki accidentally blinded himself with his own sai. This wasn't like her at all.

Kanna finally got herself under control. Her face flushed, she wiped tears from her cheeks. "God, Nick, all this time, you really—" She trailed off into another giggling fit.

"Kanna, I don't understand. I killed Master Kikuchi, and—"

"No, you didn't."

"I didn't?"

"No, see," Kanna took his arm, her demeanor suddenly serious, "That day, Dad didn't show for breakfast. I found him in his chambers with a concussion. He couldn't remember much. Kept asking, *where's Nick, where's Nick?* We looked all over, couldn't find you anywhere. After a while, I thought . . ."

"What?"

"You got tired of being a ninja and left. I knew you always wanted to be a chef, hell, that's why Dad made up that whole *Chosen One* nonsense—"

"Wait, what?"

"—But I always thought if you ran away, you'd ask me to come with you."

Nick leaned a hand against the wall, feeling very, very tired. "Kanna, if I was only running away I totally would have asked you to come with me."

"You would?"

"I never would have left you, unless . . . " He took her hands in his. They stared into each other's eyes, and suddenly it felt like no time had passed at all, they were back in Mie Prefecture, racing through the trees, cherry blossoms falling and filling the air with their sweet, pungent scent—

Kanna leaned in and kissed him.

The gesture floored him, harder than any blow, and for a moment the only thing that existed in the entire universe was her lips on his, her warmth, her scent—

Kanna pulled away. "I really want to do a lot more of that, like a LOT more, but we're standing in a sewer and this dickhead ninja is about to take over the fifth or sixth biggest city in the United States, sooooo?"

"Yeah, me, uh—same." Nick's head still reeled, both from the kiss and from the revelations. For a decade he'd harbored the guilt and shame of killing Master Kikuchi, at the same time fearing he was such a buffoon he might accidentally kill his new master, Pierre. And now, learning that everything he knew was wrong, he felt both free and afraid.

Who the FUCK was he?

But more importantly—

"Wait," Nick said. "Does this mean Master Kikuchi is, is—"

Kanna's face fell. "No."

"But if I didn't kill him, then—"

"Saru," Kanna spat. "Not long after you left. He

poisoned my father, total bitch move, and then stole the Sticks of Heaven. Some from our Clan joined up with him. He killed the others."

"Except you."

"I've been hunting him ever since. But it's not about revenge anymore. Saru's dangerous. Power-mad. He wants the whole world under his heel, we gave to stop him."

Anger welled up inside Nick. All these years he'd been punishing himself for something that asshole Saru did? "I'm in. For more than a business license. Saru's got to pay for what he's done."

Kanna hugged him tightly. "Good. Let's go kill that shitty monkey-douche. But first—" She pulled a pair of nunchucks from her shinobi shōzoku. "You ready for these?"

"Where did you—"

"Grabbed 'em from the car, right before that bullshit with the cement. I didn't know what your deal was, Nick." She pressed the nunchucks into his hand. "But I knew you'd come around."

Nick took the nunchaku, stepped back, flexing the length of the chain. He gave them a quick spin. All these years later, the motion still conjured up the vestigial memory of the incredibly brief moment he'd wielded the Sticks of Heaven, the sheer exhilaration simply *holding* the ultimate weapon of Orenji-iro no Kame brought. These nunchaku certainly weren't the Sticks of Heaven.

But they'd do fine.

"We should hurry," Nick said. "We've got a mayoral coup to stop. Except, which way's the airfield?"

Something rustled in the shadows, bigger than any rat.

Nick and Kanna spun simultaneously, weapons at the ready.

"Reveal yourself!" Kanna commanded.

"Uh, hi." A schlumpy guy stepped out of the shadows, shoulders hunched. If he was one of Saru's ninjas in disguise, they were really playing the long game. "You aren't with those bad ninjas, are you?"

"No. Who are you?" Kanna asked.

"Doug Frederson," the man said. "Water Department. No, wait," he drew himself upright, his visage resolute, "The Water *and* Sewage Department. Know these tunnels like the back of my hand. I heard you're trying to get to the airfield?"

"We are," Kanna said.

"I can take you there. On one condition."

"What?" Nick asked.

The man tucked his thumbs in his overalls. "You're going to do something about those bad ninjas, right?"

Kanna grinned. "Oh, we're going to kill the *shit* out of them."

GO NINJA GO NINJA GO

NICK GRUNTED, trying to maintain his balance on the ladder and heft the heavy manhole cover aside. Luckily, Kanna noticed his struggle and braced his calves, letting him concentrate on shoving aside two-hundred-and-fifty fucking pounds of straight-up (imported) Turbo City steel with zero leverage.

"Huh!" Nick cried, muscles burning. The manhole cover screeched, lifted a quarter inch, more. Sweat ran down his brow, his arms shook, but he pushed *hard* and tossed the cover aside. It clattered to the ground a few inches away. Sunlight streamed through the open hole.

"That was hot," Kanna said.

Nick turned back to Kanna, and the strangely-normal man they'd met in the sewer. "Twenty minutes to spare. We couldn't have done it without your help, Doug."

The man shrugged humbly. "Please, call me Doug."

"I did."

"Sorry, I'm not used to it. Everyone else on the Turbo City Secret Council calls me Shitboy, and my wife—"

"Why do they call you Shitboy?" Kanna asked.

"Because they're not your friends," Nick said, "We are. We'll never forget you, Mr. Fredericksburg. Put her there." He held onto the top rung with one hand, extended his other to Doug.

The City Water and Sewage Manager gave his hand a manly squeeze, then shook hands with Kanna. "Good luck," Doug Frederson said.

"Hide out down here for a while," Kanna said. "Things are going to get crazier before they get better."

"I'll take that under advisement."

Nick pulled himself out of the manhole and immediately rolled right, flattening himself against the ground. He was in the middle of a huge field, no cover in sight. Maybe fifty yards away, the blimp hangar nearly blocked out the sun—a massive concrete and corrugated metal structure, four stories tall, dwarfing the control tower behind it.

Kanna popped out of the hole, manriki at the ready. "Uh-oh."

"That's what I said. Make a run for it?"

"Yep!" Kanna broke into a sprint.

Nick followed, catching up to her in a few quick strides. He didn't see anyone about, but the hangar was surely crawling with ninjas, not to mention Saru himself. Chances of them making it undetected were slim to none. Any moment, he expected a fusillade of arrows, shuriken, and douchebag cheaterpants automatic weapons fire to be unleashed.

Even so.

The nunchucks felt good in his hands—scratch that, fucking great—and running with Kanna, the wind in his hair and the rising thrum of impending battle in his heart?

Well, SHIT, man.

Half the distance to go. The Kong-sized doors were cracked open a few dozen feet, but they revealed nothing more than a thin slice of darkness. Nick and Kanna ran faster, crossing the ground as quickly as they could, the hangar getting closer—

"Hai!" A dozen ninjas poured out of the open doors, swinging swords, pulling bowstrings, spinning sais like sixguns. Taking up a position in front of the door, the message clear.

You trynna get up in this bitch?

You gonna have to go through these motherfuckers RIGHT CHERE.

"I got this!" Nick yelled.

"Nick, wait!"

He bolted past her, charging right at the waiting ninjas.

Arrows flew, but he swung the nunchucks and easily shattered the shafts. He flipped over a few shuriken and landed in the midst of the ninjas.

Nunchucks spun, snapped, twirled, a Tasmanian fucking Devil bolted onto the hands of the man named Nunchuck "Nick" Nikolopoulos.

Cartilage crunched, bones broke, skulls cracked.

Grown-ass ninjas cried like straight up BITCHES, yo.

Nick snapped the nunchucks behind his back, striking his best Bruce Lee pose. The ground was littered with the bodies of twelve broken ninjas, some still whimpering softly, others silenced forever.

"Holy shit," Kanna said, catching up to Nick.

Nick grabbed one of the few surviving ninjas by the neck, hoisted him into the air. "How many more of you assholes are in there?"

The ninja spat in his face. "The master will kill you!"

"Ew." Nick tossed the ninja away like a crumpled-up burrito wrapper, wiped at the spit with his forearm.

Kanna whisked her ninjato out and ended Spitty's insolent, expectorative existence with a single SPLUCH. "They know we're here." She indicated the hangar with her bloody ninjato. "Might as well take the front do—"

A strange droning sound filled the air. Nick and Kanna exchanged leery glances.

Lights flashed inside the hangar.

Nick and Kanna backed up, circling away from the door until they were back-to-back.

"Be ready—"

KZZZT! GRZZZT! BRZZZZZZT!

Something vaguely ninja-shaped exited the building, except it was wrapped in a metal exoskeleton, steel cables snaking all over its body, and a bug-eyed and light-studded apparatus atop its head.

"What the shit is that?"

The Cyber-Ninja pointed a glistening metal claw at Nick and made the universal sign for *get over here and throw down, bitch.*

"I'm here, too," Kanna said, rolling her eyes.

Nick gave the Cyber-Ninja an instant once-over. Despite the wicked-looking exoskeleton, plenty of soft spots still lay exposed. A few well-placed nunchuck thwacks would reduce the souped-up assassin to a busted-up flesh-sack in a gaudy metal suit.

KRRRZZZT! BZZZT!

More Cyber-Ninjas streamed out of the hangar, taking up position alongside the first one. A dozen, two dozen—

"This is not good," Nick said, backing away.

Kanna gulped. "If we run back to the sewer, we'll have an advantage. Fight them as they come down the manhole."

"If we can—"

"DIEEEEEEEEEEEEEEEEEEEEEEEEEEEEEEEE EEEEEE!" One of the Cyber-Ninjas screamed, the hangar door sliding shut behind them.

"Ruuuuuuunnn," Kanna replied, bolting back towards the sewer.

Nick took off behind her.

Something BRRRZZZTED behind him. Dark shapes blotted out the sky. Cyber-Ninjas soared above, bootjets rocketing them over Nick and Kanna's heads. They landed in front of the open manhole, dropping back into fighting position, BRRRZTing and clanking and flashing their lights menacingly.

Kanna pulled up short, spinning her manriki.

Nick whirled towards the hangar, standing back-to-back with Kanna.

The other Cyber-Ninjas spread themselves out in a wide circle. They were completely surrounded.

"I'd give my left hand for an EMP right now," Kanna muttered.

"Maybe we can break through their line—"

"Doubt it." She grabbed his wrist, gave it a tight squeeze. "I'm glad we found each other again. I love you, you big fucking goofball."

Nick's heart hitched, tears threatened to come

streaming down his cheeks. From a young age, Master Kikuchi had prepared them all to die in battle. He'd expected his life might end like this, up until he'd accidentally not-actually killed the master and fled. But all the times he'd imagined his death, never once had he thought to picture the love of his life by his side.

"Love you too," Nick managed.

"Whatever happens next, I'm going to find you. You're not getting away from me again."

Nick smiled tightly, watching the Cyber-Ninjas close in—slowly, savoring the tender morsels they'd caught in their technological douche-trap. "Not if I find you first."

"On three, we go down fighting. One, two—"

"Stop!" a voice cried.

Nick searched for the source of the voice, spotted a woman with long black hair and two tekagi-shuko on either hand striding across the tarmac. She moved quickly, closing the distance to the hemmed-up real ninjas and the asshole Cyber-Ninjas in seconds.

"Sasayaku," Kanna said quietly.

"Who?"

"After your time."

The woman strode past the Cyber-Ninjas, entering the makeshift circle. "Kanna Kikuchi. I've been looking for you."

"Same," Kanna said.

Sasayaku smirked. "Guess we both win. Yaaaaaaaaay."

"You should have stayed in the hangar. Let your goons do your dirty work."

"Oh please, you know I'm a real claws-on kind of

girl." Sasayaku scraped her tekagi-shuko together, sparks bursting off the claws.

"Since you're so fucking DIY, how about a deal? Let Nick go, and I'll fight you one-on-one. If I win, I'll surrender to your men."

"I can live with that."

Nick gasped. "Kanna, no—"

Kanna turned to him. "Nick, it's the only way. We're outnumbered, Saru's won. If one of us gets away, at least there's a chance that months, years from now, *someone* can get revenge for Clan Hanasu Nezumi."

"It should be you."

Kanna smiled sadly. "You're the Chosen One, Nick."

"You told me there was no such thing."

"There wasn't. I'm choosing you now. You *are* Clan Hanasu Nezumi, as long as you draw breath—"

"Oh, will you two shut up already?" Sasayaku spat. "Let's do this."

"First, let Nick go."

Sasayaku motioned to the Cyber-Ninjas blocking the manhole. They KRRRZZTed out of the way.

The manhole awaited Nick. A round, smelly promise of freedom. And a future.

One that seemed particularly drab and dull without Kanna. Surely he'd become one of those crotchety, bitter ninjas, squatting in a rat-infested flat down at the docks or something, drinking away his problems until a chance encounter with a young kid who'd been bullied at school, and he'd take the child under his wing, teach them the long-forgotten ways of Clan Hanasu Nezumi, and then die in his sleep just before his student realizes the real power isn't ninjutsu, it's believing in themselves.

"Go, Nick."

Nick took a sullen step towards the manhole. Another. Couple more and he'd drop back down into that subterranean world where he'd had the scales pulled from his eyes minutes before.

Only this time, he wouldn't be learning anything good about himself.

KANNA VS. SASAYAKU

SASAYAKU WAVED A claw at Kanna. "Come on, bitch. No more stalling, let's see what you've got."

Kanna gripped the manriki tightly. She possessed the reach advantage, but Sasayaku was quick, deadly in the clinch, and got off on pain. If she kept her distance, she could win. And even though winning meant being torn apart by a bunch of asshole Cyber-Ninjas, sending that claw-handed cunt to Hell first would be worth it.

Sasayaku circled, a predatory gleam in her eye.

Kanna mirrored her movements, waiting for the perfect moment to strike. Thoughts of Nick tugged at her, but she couldn't indulge them. Not until she'd—

"Aiiiii!" Nick sailed through the air, swinging his nunchucks.

Sasayaku cocked her head towards the new threat—

Nick's blow landed, staving in the woman's head with a sickening CRUNCH. She teetered and fell over, her face a mess of blood and shattered bone, one eye hanging loose down her cheek. Laid on the ground, unmoving.

Nick rolled, let momentum carry him into one of

the Cyber-Ninjas, nunchucking his knees. Kneecaps popped, leaving the ninja flailing uselessly at the air with his arms, suspended in a nigh-unbreakable exoskeleton driven by haptic sensors.

Kanna didn't have time to curse the valiant, boneheaded, futile and momentarily-ass-saving play. She zipped her manriki at the closest Cyber-Ninja and ripped some cables loose. The exoskeleton sparked angrily.

Two more Cyber-Ninja jumped her, she pulled her ninjato and impaled one through the stupidly-exposed squishy bits, intestines flopping free, then decapitated the other.

Nick was back on his feet, nunchucks whipping this way and that, obliterating sensory arrays and crushing limbs. Metal claws raked his back, but he flipped away and snapped another Cyber-Ninja's neck with a brutal blow to the base of the skull.

"Nick! The hangar!" They could at least prevent the ninjas from surrounding them completely with a wall at their backs.

Something heavy crashed into Kanna, sending her spinning to the ground. A Cyber-Ninja loomed over her, claws descending.

Kanna thrust the ninjato into the space under its chin. Blood sprayed her face. She rolled out of the way just before her attacker dropped.

Nick kneecapped another Cyber-Ninja, smashed the next in its bug-eyed headgear, blinding it. The Cyber-Ninja spun around, keening wildly. Nick jumped on its back, wrapped the nunchucks around its throat, and squeezed.

"Go to the hangar, NOW!"

The Cyber-Ninja whined, claws grasping at its neck. Nick tightened his hold, cutting off the ninja's air completely—none of that tech obviated the need to breathe.

Bootjets fired, launching them into the air.

Another Cyber-Ninja claw whooshed through the air, narrowly missing Kanna's head and tearing massive divots out of the ground. She whipped the manriki at the Cyber-Ninja Nick had commandeered, the chain wrapping around its ankle. In a microsecond the slack went out of the line and she was pulled through a cloud of swiping claws. One tore her shinobi shōzoku, but she choked up on the manriki, and then she was flying through the air towards the hangar.

A cry rose up from the remaining Cyber-Ninja, a cacophony of displeased GRRRZZTs. They sped towards the side of the hangar, the ground twenty feet below. As they reached it Kanna let go of the manriki and somersaulted to the tarmac.

Above her, a loud CRACK signaled the snapping of a ninja neck. An exoskeleton-clad body flopped to the ground next to her, sending up a poof of dust, followed by Nick landing on his feet, nunchucks whirling from one hand to the other.

The remaining Cyber-Ninjas charged.

Some rocketed into the air, others took fast, mechanically-assisted strides.

Still way too many left.

"You're an idiot," Kanna said with a tight smile. "But you're *my* idiot."

They braced themselves, ready to fight to the death.

THOOM! The ground shook, Nick and Kanna nearly fell over.

Nick spun around, expecting maybe a herd of dinosaurs or something.

NOPE—instead, there was a goddamn four-story tall robot ninja striding across the tarmac, complete with shiny metal shinobi shōzoku. Smoked glass shrouded what would have been the eye slits in a normal ninja's mask. MechaNinZilla came straight at them, crushing golf carts and trams beneath its metal feet like roaches.

Even the Cyber-Ninja paused in their assault, stopping to witness the oncoming apocalypse.

"Oh come the FUCK on!" Kanna cried.

JFC THIS IS A KAIJU BOOK NOW?

NICK SCOPED OUT the robotic monster, barreling towards them at an unbelievable pace for something so big. "The smoked glass has to be a cockpit. If we can get up there—"

"Too bad you killed our ride," Kanna said, motioning to the dead Cyber-Ninja next to them.

The remaining Cyber-Ninjas, who'd overcome their momentary shock at seeing a much bigger version of themselves, advanced. "Maybe we can grab another one."

"Can't believe that trick worked the first time. The hangar!"

They ran to the hangar door. No handles.

Nick pressed buttons on the keypad at random. Predictably, nothing happened. "We're locked out!"

The herd of Cyber-Ninjas got closer, the gigantic goddamn robot close behind.

"Uh oh," Nick said.

MechaNinZilla's glass visor glowed red, then a massive beam of light shot out, blotting out the sun.

BZZZZZZZZZZZZZZZZZZZZZAPPPPPPPPPPPPPP PPPP!

Nick and Kanna hit the ground, shielding their eyes, ears echoing from the laser blast. Very much expecting to be immolated.

Instead, the stench of burning metal and burning ninja filled the air.

Nick blinked, peered through his fingers. A few scorch marks, twisted metal and piles of ash were all that remained of the Cyber-Ninjas. The giant robot had come to a stop a few dozen yards away. It raised one metal hand, phone booth-sized fingers pressed tight together.

And waved.

"What the fuck," Kanna said.

A compartment in the robot's chest opened, revealing a well-dressed Indian woman and an overmuscled Duffman cosplayer.

"Hello," the woman said over a loudspeaker. "I'm Lakshmi Rao, CEO of Turbo Tech. This is Chad Boner, Chief Bikini Inspector."

"This is the dumbest fucking city on the planet," Kanna muttered.

Chad Boner gave them a long-distance fist bump. "Sup. Also, boobs."

Nick and Kanna exchanged very confused glances.

"I must apologize," Lakshmi said, "For my technology." The robot pointed at the remains of the Cyber-Ninjas. "The man you seek stole it from me."

"Such a dick," Kanna said. "How'd you find us?"

Lakshmi shrugged. "I put nano-trackers in all my tech."

"Thanks for the save," Kanna said. "We're going to go kill Kundarai Saru now."

"And save the mayor-dude?" Chad Boner asked.

"That's part of it, yes."

"We can help you," Lakshmi said. "He's in the hangar?"

Kanna nodded.

"Stand back, please."

The compartment zipped closed. MechaNinZilla quickly crossed the tarmac to the hangar, the ground rumbling with every step.

Nick and Kanna moved out of the way, stepping over cremated Cyber-Ninjas, and took up a position to the side. The robot sank its hands into the roof, a screeching sound filling the air. The robot tore off a chunk the size of a gas station and tossed it over its shoulder, landing on some distant section of the tarmac like a goddamn meteor, then went in for another piece.

"This is safe, right? They're not going to make the whole thing collapse?" Kanna said.

"Maybe?"

The robot finished tearing the roof of the building, and somehow the walls still stood. Momentarily, at least. The robot leaned over the open-air hangar, then turned back to Nick and Kanna, the driver's compartment opening up again.

"We've got a problem," Lakshmi said. "Here, come see."

The robot sank to its knees, a hand opening on the ground in front of Nick and Kanna.

"Guess we get to ride a robot today," Kanna said. "Had not expected that." She stepped into the robot's palm.

Nick followed, slightly uneasy. If the robot so much as flexed its hand, they'd be crushed to death.

Although, Lakshmi could have easily lasered them to death like the Cyber-Ninjas.

Suddenly they were rising into the air. Nick's head swum sickeningly with the rapid motion, the horizon canting at an odd angle. He braced himself against a robo-joint and tried to enjoy the ride.

Kanna looked completely at ease, like riding robo-palms was just this thing she did.

They rose above the towering walls of the hangar, crept to the edge of the palm to get a good look.

The place was empty.

Nick searched the darkest corners of the hangar, looking for hiding places, but there were none—one cavernous room, big enough to hold a piece-of-shit blimp, and little else.

"Where's Saru?"

Kanna slammed a fist down on the robot. "I thought for sure, I mean why would he have all those Cyber-Ninjas here if . . . " She trailed off, a confused and angry look contorting her face.

Nick glanced at his watch.

4:58.

They were screwed.

In two minutes, Kundarai Saru was going to beat the ever-living shit out of the mayor, take his job, and institute a brutal ninjocracy in Turbo City. Nick would never get to open a fondue restaurant with his best friend Rondell, and if he was smart should probably get the fuck out of town, since Saru wouldn't appreciate any ninja-shaped loose ends lying around.

"Guess it's over," Nick mumbled, sinking into the giant robot's palm.

Kanna sat down next to him, rested her head on

his shoulder. "We can go somewhere else. Anywhere. They say living well's the best revenge. I never believed that bullshit, but it wouldn't hurt to try. Maybe you can take me to France, introduce me to Pierre."

"I'd like that." Nick stood, extending a hand to Kanna, pulling her up. "Guess we should tell Lakshmi to set—"

A loud screech rent the sky.

Nick looked up. The blimp circled overhead, the loudspeakers squelching static. The screen on the side of the blimp flickered, resolved into a close-up of Saru's shitty face.

Saru backed away from the camera and said, "Turbo City! Your time has come. In one minute, I'm going to kick the shit out of your leader. And then you'll be calling *me* Mr. Mayor." He held a finger to his lips. "Actually, I might adopt a new title. How does *Shogun* Mayor sound?"

"Definitely got a ring to it," an off-screen voice said.

Saru blanched. "Daisuke, I swear to—" He collected himself, turned back to the camera. "Let's begin."

Two ninjas wheeled Mayor DiFormaggio out from behind a curtain, still duct-taped to a chair. He looked frantic, hair plastered to his forehead, and had clearly pissed himself several times.

"Cut him loose," Saru said. "This must be a fair fight."

"Nick!" Kanna said, tapping his arm and pointing at the blimp. "He's not in the hangar. He's been in the blimp this whole time."

"How're we going to get up there?" Nick asked.

"Allow me!" Lakshmi called from below. Another compartment on the robot's back opened, deploying a large cylinder that looked sort of like a jet engine.

"Hold onto your tits and/or dicks!" Chad yelled.

Nick and Kanna wrapped themselves around a robo-finger.

Then the jet pack roared and they took off into the sky.

MEANWHILE, AT THE SMOKING CRATER THAT USED TO BE A FONDUE RESTAURANT

RONDELL BLINKED.
The simple, parasympathetic action blew his mind. He'd probably blinked a hundred million times, never thought twice about it, but now every blink seemed like a gift.

He was dimly aware of the scorched corpse on top of him, the sickening reek of charred flesh and hair, the ringing in his ears. The important thing was blinking. In between blinks, he stared up at the blue, blue sky where the roof used to be and marveled at the fact that he could see anything at all.

Eventually, the novelty of blinking wore off, like it does for most people over the age of six weeks. Rondell held his breath and shoved the corpse away, then staggered to his feet.

Fond Dudes was donezo.

The door to the walk-in hung by its hinges, the steel on one side burned black. Only a skeletal suggestion of the building's frame remained, crumpled steel posts reaching crookedly up at the sky. Patches of flame still crackled amidst piles of debris.

He ran a hand through his hair, over his face. Looked down at his body, his legs. His clothes were singed, but overall the dead guy with the ninja star stuck in his head had done a pretty good job of sheltering Rondell from the worst of the blast. Rondell made a mental note to track down the guy's family, hook them up with some coupons for free drinks whenever he got Fond Dudes rebuilt.

And he would. He fucking would. Sure, the insurance company would bitch and moan about fulfilling the claim, since technically Rondell blew up his own restaurant, but with the extenuating circumstances a highly-paid legal team could easily net him a few million.

"Aw, shit!" someone yelled. A pile of twisted metal in the former kitchen shifted. "That was one cracker of a kablooey."

Rondell screamed, stumbled over the dead guy, landing on his ass.

KRONG! The pile of scrap metal shifted again. Slag rose from the heap, one side of his face blackened, an arm missing, the jagged bone poking out of a mass of charred flesh. He wavered, like a punch-drunk boxer, and pointed most of a finger at Rondell.

"Thought you could explodearoo old Slag, could ya? I been blown up by the best, and you, sonny, are far from it!"

Rondell wanted to run, but the ass-end of the walk-in was still intact, somehow. The only way out was past the horrifically injured sumo.

The ninja star still glinted in the back of the dead man's head. Rondell grabbed it, stabbing the webbing of his hand. Grunting, he wrenched the ninja star free.

A shitty weapon, and he didn't know how to use it. But Slag was injured, grievously. If he could hold his own for a few minutes—

"Time to die," Slag said, grabbing a burnt piece of rebar.

"Oh yeah?" Rondell said, holding up the shuriken. "You better back off, or I'll shove this ninja star up your ass!"

Slag grinned. "Good luck, me bum is sealed up tigher'n a baby kanga's coocharooney." He slapped the rebar against his stomach. "And, you've just given me a bright idea for this little beaut."

"I mean it!" Rondell yelled, waving the ninja star in what he hoped was a menacing or at least mildly competent manner. "I'll—"

"You'll what, then? Here, I'll give you a free shot. Again."

Rondell squeezed the ninja star tight. He'd seen guys do this in movies. A flick of the wrist, he could blind the sumo, and then hopefully slip by him.

"You got this," Rondell whispered.

Aimed at Slag's remaining eye.

And threw!

The shuriken sailed end-over-end towards Slag's face, a whirling dervish of destruction—

CLANG! Slag knocked it aside with the rebar, the shuriken spinning off-course and lodging in the wall.

"Shit," Rondell said. Out of weapons, he put up his dukes, ready to go down fighting.

Slag pointed the rebar at him. "Say g'bye to your thinkin' box—"

WHIRRRRRRRRRRRRRRRRRRR!

Slag frowned, twisting around in an effort to locate the odd sound.

Rondell peered over Slag's shoulder, into the smoking remains of the restaurant. A mummy-like creature sat there, maybe ten feet behind Slag. Rondell gaped at the sight, blinked a couple times.

Not a mummy.

A man, or maybe a woman, wearing a full-body cast and seated in an electric wheelchair.

And, most importantly, holding two bolt-action crossbows in either cast-covered hand.

"Who the fuck're you supposed to be?" Slag snarled.

"I'm Skip Baxter, the Most Dangerous Man in Turbo City," the cast-covered figure said. "And *these* are my deadly weapons!"

SHUCK!

One crossbow fired, the bolt shooting straight into Slag's good eye and punching out the back of his skull, showering Rondell with blood, brain matter and bone fragments.

The sumo roared, swinging the rebar blindly. The metal bar glanced off the wrecked door frame, bouncing back and pounding the bolt further into his brain. Slag's roar became a wail.

Skip Baxter fired his other crossbow.

The bolt shot through Slag's throat, cutting off the big man's cries. Slag dropped the rebar, remaining hand clutching at his throat, before he collapsed to the ground.

His body jerked a few times, then lay still.

Rondell gaped. "The fuck?"

"Don't thank me," Skip Baxter said. "All in a day's work."

"No, I'm definitely thanking you. Thank you!"

"You're welcome. Now, uh, could you help me out with a reload?"

Rondell scrambled around the dead sumo. He quickly found the bag of bolts slung on the back of the wheelchair, and with a little coaching got both crossbows reloaded.

"There's more of them out there," Skip said. "I could use someone to watch my six."

Rondell looked at the remains of his newest restaurant, immolated mere days before its grand opening. Maybe Slag was dead, but if there were still other assholes out there, doing bullshit like this?

He could at least make sure they burned down his competition.

Rondell grabbed the piece of rebar off the ground and pointed at the emergency exit, which was now a big hole. "Let's do the damn thing."

PRELUDE TO AN ASS-WHUPPING

MAYOR JOE DIFORMAGGIO pissed himself yet again when the ninjas came for him, pulling him unceremoniously out of a closet and shoving him roughly into their makeshift studio.

Now, with the strange blonde-haired man in a silk bathrobe mugging for the camera, talking about a bunch of things Mayor Joe didn't understand, he felt the urge to piss himself one last time, but all he could manage was a dry, urethral spasm. They really should have given him some water. If he ever had the chance to write a Yelp review of his kidnapping, he couldn't imagine giving the ninjas more than a single, paltry star.

Eh, maybe one-and-a-half—Mayor Joe didn't want to treat any Turbo City-based business *too* critically, even if said business tied him to a chair and left him to stew in his own piss-pants for hours on end. The Chamber of Commerce would make his life a living hell. He'd rather spend all day in a dark closet than deal with Myrna Grable, the city's business liaison. Myrna had some very firm ideas about what constituted ethical behavior vis a vis Turbo City's elected officials and its myriad businesses (rezoning an empty lot to prevent an out-of-town hardware chain from moving in was kosher, but writing a negative review of Screw City after the owner chased him out of the store with a 2x4 was not).

"Cut him loose," the blonde bathrobe guy said. "This must be a fair fight."

Two ninjas sliced through Mayor Joe's bonds. He was free! He rose shakily to his feet, adjusted his *Miss Turbo City 2014* sash, and immediately ran for the back door. He wrenched the door open, revealing a small, dark compartment filled with ninjas. Mayor Joe screamed, turned around and ran straight into the head kidnapper.

"Let's do this," Saru said, cracking his knuckles.

Mayor Joe's bladder wheezed dust out the tip of his dick.

NICK & KANNA VS. KUNDARAI SARU

BORNE IN THE palm of a massive ninja-shaped robot with a goddamn jet pack, Nick and Kanna clung on tightly and watched the blimp get closer and closer.

Or, more specifically the gondola, a bus-shaped structure clinging to the blimp's underbelly like a tick. Windows lined the gondola, but they were blacked-out with drapes—Saru's makeshift TV studio.

"Let's go in the back!" Kanna yelled over the drone of MechaNinZilla's jet pack, a droning roar that gave Nick a serious jaw ache and stressed his mediocre lip-reading skills.

Nick waved his assent. The back of the gondola looked to have an entrance. They could sneak in, hopefully catch Saru off-guard, or at least without the Sticks of Heaven close at hand.

If Saru had truly mastered the Sticks, they didn't stand a chance.

The robot's retro-jets fired, slowing their ascent. The gondola's ass-end neared. Nick relaxed his grip on the robo-finger, got ready to jump.

"Ready?" he mouthed at Kanna.

In response, she pantomimed kicking the air, which Nick inferred to be a stand-in for Kundarai Saru's stank ass.

"Let's do this!"

Nick ran across the robot's palm, reached the edge, and jumped.

He sailed through the air, high above Turbo City, and jump-kicked the shit out of the gondola door. The door easily gave way, crashing inward. Nick rolled, popping up to his feet in a small compartment.

Two ninjas pounced from either side.

Nick spun his nunchucks, smacking one ninja under the chin, whipping them back the other way to pound the other ninja across the bridge of the nose, snapping cartilage with a gunshot crack.

Kanna flipped in through the open door, grabbed the nose-broke ninja by the shinobi shōzoku and booted them the fuck out of the blimp.

The other ninja recovered, pulled a knife.

Nick knocked the knife aside and fractured the ninja's skull with another nunchuck blow. The body crumpled to his feet.

"Saru must be through here," Nick said, rearing back and kicking the next door open.

Light streamed in through the doorway. Nick rushed into the next compartment, a much bigger space.

Saru stood at the far end, squaring off with the mayor, a mewling shrimp of a man in a sash that read *Miss Turbo City 2014*.

"Saru!" Nick yelled. "Leave the mayor alone!"

Saru turned to him. "Nunchuck Nick. What a surprise."

Kanna flipped into the main cabin. "You're finished, Saru!"

Saru winked. "Oh, I'm just getting started."

Spun.

And nailed Mayor Joe in the grill with a left hook.

The mayor hit the floor like the bitch-ass politician he was.

"Whoop!" Saru yelled, fist-pumping the air. "You got that, right?"

The ninja cameraman in the corner gave a thumbs-up.

Saru turned back to Nick. "Ha! *I'm* the mayor now. One sec." He bent down, ripped the sash off the prone public servant, donned it himself. Saru clenched the sash between a thumb and forefinger and felt it up, pervert-style. "Ahh. This feels nice. And, you can't do a thing. This is all legal. You fuck with me, you're fucking with one of America's mayors. And you know America isn't going to like that."

Nick's heart sank. They'd come so far, only to see Saru succeed with his devious plan by a matter of seconds. Maybe if they'd reached the blip a minute earlier, things would've—

"Psst, Nick," Kanna said out the side of her mouth.

Saru was too busy pacing the length of the cabin and pumping his fists in the air to notice.

"What?"

"That stupid rule they made? Krueger's Law?"

"*Kurgan*'s Law. Krueger's Law made it illegal to murder a janitor in a boiler room."

"Whatever. Point is, if he can kick the mayor's ass and become the mayor, why can't *we* kick his ass and become the next mayor?"

Nick's jaw dropped. Of course they could. And then he could sign his *own* business license.

"Saru!" Nick yelled, leveling an index finger at the celebrating douche.

Saru stopped mid-fist pump. "What? I'm in the middle of some really important mayor stuff. You wouldn't understand."

"Oh, I think we will," Kanna said. "Right after we kick—"

"YOUR."

"ASS!"

Saru laughed. "The two of you? The ghosts of a dead clan? You. Are. NOTHING!"

Nick took a step forward. "Let me ask you something."

"Ha! Please."

"How many friends do you have?"

Saru scratched his chin. "Friends?"

"See, I've got three," Nick said. "Kanna, Rondell, and Dave."

"Doug," Kanna clarified.

"And I guess Pierre, but he's really more of a master than a friend."

"Who cares?" Saru sneered.

"My point," Nick said, tucking his nunchucks under his arm, "You've got nothing to fight for but yourself. But me? I've got three different reasons to kick your ass! Hai!"

Nick lunged, whipping the nunchucks out from under his arm.

Saru dodged away. "Guess it's time you meet *my* friends!" With a flourish he pulled the Sticks of Heaven from the folds of his kimono. Eldritch energies erupted from the ancient weapons of Orenji-iro no Kame, crackling up Saru's arms.

The light grew horribly bright, Nick shielded his eyes with a forearm, staggered back into Kanna. "What's—what's happening?"

"Shinji rarenai," Kanna said softly. "He really did master the Sticks."

A cocoon of blazing yellow energy surrounded Saru, his figure a vague outline within the miasma of power. The pressure inside the cabin swelled. Nick clenched his jaw in pain, something throbbed behind his eyes.

Then the windows shattered.

Wind whooshed into the gondola, buffeting its occupants.

"Screw this," said the Camera-Ninja, grabbing a parachute from a compartment next to his camera and bailing out the back.

"You thought you could challenge *me?*" Saru yelled from somewhere inside the energy ball. "Your own father named me *Glorious Warrior*! Right before I killed him."

"It means shitty monkey!" Kanna yelled.

The light ceased crackling, the energy fading, Saru's frowny face becoming visible. "What?"

"Kuda-ran-ai," Kanna said, speaking loudly and slowly, "means *shitty* in Japanese. And *Saru* means monkey. My father named you *shitty monkey* because you have a terrible attitude and weird-ass arms, but you couldn't even pronounce it, kept calling yourself *Kundarai*. That's not even a word!"

Saru scoffed. "I'm pretty sure I know what my own name means, sweetheart."

"Kay. If you're so fluent in Japanese, how do you say *I'm a stupid idiot who doesn't know what my own nickname means?*"

"Why would I say that?"

While Saru and Kanna were talking, Nick snuck around the edge of the room. If she could keep him talking, maybe he could make a play for the Sticks. Without the ultimate weapon, Saru was just another asshole who knew a middling amount of ninjutsu and mainly relied on a cadre of well-paid henchmen to get by.

"Okay, fine. Here's an easy one. Say *I am riding in a blimp.*"

Saru shook his head. "I don't want to." The energy field continued to fade—the Sticks of Heaven must have been getting bored with the moronic back-and-forth.

"Don't want to, or *can't* want to?" Kanna had her hands on her hips, head cocked to the side.

"Can't want to? What does that even mean?"

Nick closed the distance silently. Saru's attention was entirely on Kanna. Who knew the best way to distract a ninja was to ask him what words mean?

"Don't worry about what it means, shitty monkey."

"Stop calling me that!" Saru's voice took on a high-pitched whine. The energy had almost entirely dissipated, except for the odd spark rippling in the folds of his kimono.

"Tell you what," Kanna said, stepping to the side, forcing Saru to crane his head even further away from Nick's direction. "If you can say *one thing* in Japanese, I'll never call you *shitty monkey* again."

"Fine. What?"

Nick was a few feet away, his approach silenced by the wind rushing in through the broken windows. The Sticks of Heaven dangled from Saru's hands, nearly forgotten in the argument with Kanna. If he were smart, he could've unleashed the full power of Orenji-iro no Kame and destroyed them both.

"Say *ambush*."

Saru laughed. "That's an easy one. Mach—"

Nick lunged for the Sticks—

And straight up tripped over Mayor DiFormaggio's prone form.

Nick fell forward, hitting the floor.

Saru jumped back, bumping into the wall, and raised the Sticks of Heaven high. "Behold, my final form! O shiri no nioi ga suru!"

Saru erupted in a blaze of light that slammed Nick and Kanna into the walls of the gondola. Nick crumpled to the ground, the wind knocked out of him.

"Oh, shit."

BOSS FIGHT 2:
EVEN BOSSIER

NICK BLINKED SLOWLY, head still fuzzed from his collision with the gondola wall. Saru was gone. In his place stood a ridiculously-proportioned caricature of a human—steroid-pumped Mr. Universe physique, glowing skin, spiked blonde hair jutting three feet off his skull. His eyes were blank, white voids. He wore nothing but a pair of grotesquely-bulging bright red hakama trousers.

Kundarai Saru was literally tumescent with power.

"Behold!" Super-Saru cried, flexing unnecessarily. "The true power of Orenji-iro no Kame!"

"So the secret of the Sticks of Heaven is they'll turn you into a giant douchebag?" Kanna said.

"Mock all you like," Super-Saru replied. "The Sticks have turned me into the ultimate version of myself."

Kanna cut him off with a battle cry, charging across the length of the gondola. She leapt into the air, swinging her ninjato.

Super-Saru moved like a blur, easily knocking her aside. Kanna bounced off the wall and fell to the floor next to Nick.

"Shit," she said, sucking in hard-fought breaths. "He's fast."

"I've got this," Nick said, jumping to his feet. He flipped and did a quick handspring off the floor, the mystical nunchucks whipping over his head, and caught Super-Saru in the chest with a dropkick.

His knees screamed in pain, he fell to the floor.

Kicking Super-Saru was like kicking eighty-seven concrete walls at once. Forty or fifty, Nick could smash right through, but eighty-seven?

NOPE.

"Hahaha," Super-Saru cackled. "You are helpless against me. I could kill you now, but what's the point?" He turned, banged on the door to the cockpit. "Driver! Take us down."

"I'm a *pilot,*" said a muffled voice from behind the door.

"Who cares?"

The pilot mumbled something and then the gondola pitched forward.

Nick grabbed onto a window frame, the air buffeting his face. Behind him, Kanna did the same.

"Yes," Super-Saru was saying, more to himself than either of the ninjas, "Maybe I'll keep you both around. Let you witness my complete and total domination of the world! Would you like that?"

"No," Kanna said.

"Of course not. It was a rhetorical question."

Nick glanced out the window. They were heading back to the hangar. News crews and ambulances had arrived, the tarmac was studded with cameras and EMTs and all sorts of on-lookers, drawn to the airfield by glimpses of a giant ninja robot. MechaNinZilla itself was parked next to the decapitated hangar.

Maybe the giant robot would be able to kick Super-Saru's ass. Except they were up here with him, and the robot was far down below.

"Nick," Kanna whispered—loudly, in order to be heard over the rushing air.

Nick twisted around.

She'd pulled something from her shinobi shōzoku, clasped it tightly in her hand. "I'll distract him, you get the Sticks of Heaven. If you can get one set, I know you can beat him."

Nick eyed Super-Saru, caught up in a rant about how once he ruled the world he'd get rid of fiat currency and implement the Bitcoin standard, or some such tech-broey bullshit, Nick couldn't begin to keep up with all the buzzwords. One pair of the Sticks dangled from each of Super-Saru's hands.

"Nick?"

"Go!"

Kanna leapt off the ground, opened her hand.

Super-Saru stopped mid-rant and turned to crack her a good one with the Sticks—

WHOOSH! Kanna blew metsubushi powder straight up into homeboy's face.

"Gah!" Super-Saru cried, dropping the Sticks in his right hand and pawing his burning Super-Eyes.

Nick rolled across the floor, snatched up the Sticks. Excitement coursed through his body, like he had to pee but much, much better. He popped back up, testing their weight.

It felt *really* fucking good to hold the Sticks again.

Kanna flipped backwards, landing next to him with her ninjato at the ready.

Super-Saru stumbled across the compartment, one hand over his eyes, the other swinging his remaining nunchaku with abandon. The Sticks crackled with energy, ripping holes out of the sides of the gondola. A pigeon flew in one of the open windows, flapped around the cabin spraying white shit on the walls, then said FUCK THIS and bailed.

Nick gripped his own set of Sticks, communing with the hidden power within.

"That's it," Kanna said, "the power of Orenji-iro no Kame is yours, Nick. Call it forth!"

Nick did.

Power coursed through his body, bursting out his pores, enveloping him. For a moment the world was nothing but bright and blazing light, and then all was calm—Nick himself the eye in the center of the storm. He couldn't even hear Super-Saru's screams.

Then everything came rushing back.

Kanna gaped at him. "My God, Nick. You look—"

Nick looked down at himself. From his own vantage point, he sure didn't look any different. Same dirty clothes. His skin didn't even glow. "The same," he finished.

Kanna touched his cheek. "Course you do. The Sticks of Heaven turn you into your best possible self. You had a bit of a head start on Chuckles over there."

"Grrrraaaah!" Super-Saru cried, lashing out with his nunchucks. The door to the cockpit caved in, crushing whoever was on the other side.

"Uh-oh," Nick said. "That means—"

"Nobody's flying this thing!"

The blimp lurched into a sudden, still-blimp-speed nose-dive. Super-Saru crashed into the remains of the forward compartment, Nick and Kanna were thrown through the air.

Nick hurtled towards Super-Saru, cocked back his nunchucks—

And swung!

The Sticks of Heaven smashed into Super-Saru's shitty face, the massive exchange of energy exploding in a starburst of raw, ninja power.

Then everything went white.

AFTERMATH

NICK CAME TO in the middle of a goddamn apocalypse.

He lay on his back, the flaming remains of the crashed blimp all around. The air stunk of burning blimp-skin.

He still clutched the Sticks of Heaven.

Nick got to his feet, the ground unsteady beneath him. Saru, no longer looking very super, lay a few feet away, half his face gone, the rest of his body covered in burns. The evil ninja's chest still rose and fell, lightly.

"Kanna!" Nick screamed, looking around wildly. They had somehow managed to crash into the hangar, the walls festooned with scrap metal and smoldering canvas. He began a frantic search, rifling through debris, tossing a battered door aside like it was nothing.

"Up here," Kanna shouted back.

Nick glanced up, caught her dangling from a broken strut by her tangled-up parachute. Other than her singed clothing, crazy hair and soot-covered face, she looked none the worse for wear.

"How did you—"

"Managed to grab a chute and bail out the back.

Haven't BASE-jumped in forever. Watch out." Kanna released the parachute straps and dropped to the ground. Nick limped over to her and they embraced tightly.

After a moment she pulled away. "Hold on." She walked over to Saru, a gently-wheezing crispy critter, and pulled her ninjato. "This is for my father, and everyone else. Bastard."

The ninjato swept down, severing Saru's asshole head.

Nick turned away, glad Saru was dead, but he didn't need to spend any more time looking at corpses. Except—

The mayor!

Mayor Joe DiFormaggio, or what was left of him, had been impaled on an upended forklift, his hands grasping towards the heavens.

"Poor guy," Kanna said, joining him. She walked over to the dead former mayor. "Sorry we couldn't save you," she said, and then pulled off his sash. She came back to Nick, draped the sash over his shoulders.

Other than a few streaks of blood, it was in pretty good shape.

"I don't want this," Nick said. "I'm not—"

Kanna put a finger to his lips. "Kurgan's Law, Nick. Now, kiss me, Mr. Mayor!"

Nick did.

Oh, you bet he did.

ALL DAY, SON!

THE PREFECT GETAWAY

DAISUKE HURTLED THROUGH the air, the exploding zeppelin at his back. Like the cool guy he was, he didn't look at the explosion. He was just glad he wasn't in it.

Briefly, he felt weightless, suspended over the wooded area south of City Hall, giving him time to reflect. Couldn't believe he'd wasted so many years following Kundarai Saru on all his dumb missions, when he could have been taking night classes at the adult education center, earning the certificate that would allow him to pursue his *real* dream:

Local news cameraman!

Daisuke imagined a future where he wasn't taking orders from a dickhead who'd never bothered to learn more than ten words of Japanese, one where he'd get to cover exciting events like cat shows and beach clean-ups. Maybe even ribbon-cutting ceremonies!

He got so distracted imagining his awesome future he almost forgot he was skydiving.

Daisuke pulled the cord, the parachute unfurling from his pack and yanking him back up into the sky. His stomach lurched. He sailed between two trees, the parachute sticking in their branches, coming to rest less than ten feet above the ground. Daisuke sliced

180

through the straps and vaulted to the ground.

The trees blocked his view of the sky, he could only imagine the flaming blimp chunks raining down throughout Turbo City, hopefully containing equally-flaming chunks of Kundarai Saru. And Nick and Kanna, for that matter. He didn't have anything personal against them, but better if they all burned the fuck up, so he could make a clean getaway.

And what's more, a clean start. *Need some new clo—*

A slide-whistle blew.

Daisuke dropped back into a fighting stance, cautiously searching the foliage for any sign of attackers.

Voices hummed and harmonized around him. "We are the Kerseyshire Hunting Club, Sons of Kersey are we . . ."

A small, well-dressed man with a monocle stepped out from behind a tree stump. "Nice threads. I'm afraid we'll require it in tribute."

"Tribute?" Daisuke asked.

"Why yes. This park is our territory. And you—"

"Let's murk this bitch already!"

"Cyril!" Monocle Man smiled apologetically. "Sorry. He really needs to work on his manners. Let's cut to the chase. Give us your clothes, or we'll kill you."

Daisuke pulled a knife. "You know I'm a ninja, right?"

"Ninja this," a voice sneered in a fake British accent.

Right before the axe split Daisuke's head in two.

LADY ROADKILL

SASAYAKU GROANED, rolling on the ground. Her head throbbed, her face felt like raw hamburger. Blood clouded her vision in one eye, while the other saw nothing at all.

She still couldn't quite figure out what happened. She'd had the two weak-ass ninjas outnumbered, outgunned. That Kikuchi bitch couldn't touch her in a fight. And then her moronic boyfriend came out of nowhere.

Though Sasayaku knew that was her fault. She'd been planning on sending her ninjas after him, letting them hunt him in the sewer. She should have expected he'd find a tiny shred of courage, although not enough to face her head on.

What kind of an asshole sucker-nunchucks a woman?

No matter. They were both assuredly dead now. She would have loved to tear Kanna apart with her claws, but at least she was alive.

Although why none of her men had thought to get her medical attention—

A shape loomed over her, filling her field of vision.

About goddamn time.

"Mike, got a live one over here!" The shape said.

Sasayaku blinked blood out of her eye. She didn't recognize the man, or what he was wearing. Looked like a beekeeper suit, adorned with, with—

Oh shit.

She definitely recognized the symbol on his coveralls.

After all, she'd spent her lunch hour killing a bunch of engineers sporting the same insignia.

"A live one?" someone else called back.

"Yeah. Looks like shit."

"Bag her."

"You're the boss."

Sasayaku realized the man was holding something that looked like a cattle prod.

Then it crackled and she found out yes, that's exactly what the fuck it was.

YUB NUB

THE *TURBO CITY* Promenade was absolutely packed.

From City Hall to the towering statue of Michael Dudikoff, patron saint of dumb martial arts stories, seemingly every surviving soul in Turbo City turned out for the celebration. The sun blazed high overhead, the crowd sweated their genitals off, jostling each other in hopes of catching a glimpse of the saviors of their fair municipality. Aside from the occasional whoop, the crowd was mostly subdued, in reverence for what they were about to witness.

A dazzling display of local luminaries walked out onto the stage, waving and smiling at the adoring crowd.

Chad Boner, Chief Bikini Inspector.
Lakshmi Rao, Head of Turbo Tech.
Rondell Wright, Local Business Leader.
Rhonda Meagle, City Clerk.
Skip Baxter, the Most Dangerous Man in Turbo City (who didn't technically walk, but . . .)
Kanna Kikuchi, Visiting Ninja and finally;
Nunchuck "Nick" Nikolopolous, Mayor of Turbo City.

NUNCHUCK CITY

Nick stepped up to the podium and adjusted his sash—they'd never found the actual mayoral sash, so it still read *Ms. Turbo City 2014*—and leaned into the microphone. "Uh, hi."

"HI, MAYOR NICK!" the crowd yelled back.

Nick's cheeks reddened. He still wasn't used to such honorifics. "Thanks for coming."

"THANKS FOR SAVING US!"

"I didn't save you. You saved yourselves. With the help of these fine folks up on stage with me. And especially Kanna."

Hoots and hollers filled the air. Kanna looked like she wanted to toss a smoke bomb and disappear.

"Like you, I've also lost things during the tragic past few days. My friend Rondell and I—" Nick pointed at Rondell, who waved to the crowd, "—were going to open a super awesome restaurant. Rondell blew it up, but the insurance came through, and now they're starting construction as we speak. I look forward to welcoming you to our new location sometime in the next eight to ten weeks. In the meantime, enjoy some complimentary fondue on me."

Dozens of servers in paper toques walked through the crowd, passing out cups of fondue and French bread.

"I have to tell you, though, I'm just a simple ninja/fondue chef. I'm not much of a politician." He dropped some finger quotes around *politician,* as one always should. "I'm here to announce my resignation."

"BOOOOOOOOO!" went the crowd.

Nick held up a hand. "Come on, hear me out. You've had the perfect mayor in front of you all along. Or, more accurately, beneath your feet. He's a hardworking, dedicated civil servant, and under his leadership I know Turbo City will rebuild, stronger than ever. Doug? Can you come up here?"

A grating noise filled the air. A manhole cover twenty feet from the stage slowly slid aside, and a filthy, wild-haired man crawled out of the sewers. The crowd parted as he approached the stage, though whether out of deference or odor, who's to say?

The man mounted the stage and met Nick at the podium. "Hi," he said, leaning into the mike, "I'm Doug Frederson. I manage the Water and Sewer department."

"Whoa, Shitboy!" Chad Boner said, excitedly punching Lakshmi's shoulder. "Babe, check it out, it's Shitboy."

"Shh," she whispered.

Nick stepped out from behind the podium. "When you're ready, Doug."

"Okay, if you're sure." Doug took a step forward, cocked a fist, and swung at Nick. The blow caught Nick on the chin.

While it didn't hurt, Nick did the decent thing and flopped to the ground like a professional soccer player. He pretended to be unconscious for a minute, then faux-groggily got to his feet. "That's it, folks, you all saw it. Doug kicked my ass, and by the laws of our fine city, is now the mayor. Doug, this is for you." Nick pulled his sash off and slowly, reverently, draped it over Doug's shoulders.

Doug walked over to the podium, hissing "It's

Mayor Shitboy" at Chad Boner as he went. "My fellow Turbosians," Doug began, his voice dropping several octaves to become an absolute study in gravitas, and then launched into a bunch of political platitudes which have little bearing on this story and are in no way ninja-related.

Nick made his way over to Kanna. She leaned her head on his shoulder, he draped an arm around her.

"I've got a surprise for you," Kanna said.

"A surprise?"

Kanna pointed out into the crowd, at the base of the Michael Dudikoff statue.

Nick squinted at where she was pointing, taking in every face until he saw—

"Wow, Pierre?"

The old man stood next to the statue, wearing a black skullcap and a faded Army jacket. Pierre locked eyes with Nick, voice booming in Nick's head.

My son, he said, but in French because he's Pierre, *I am very proud of you. The best fondue chefs are ninjas. Thus it has always been, and thus it will ever be.*

Then he shimmered out of existence.

"That was awesome!" Nick said. "Weird, but awesome."

Kanna laughed. "Took some doing. That guy's really hard to reach. Anyway, that's not all. I have one more surprise."

"ANOTHER one?"

"You didn't notice the second stage?"

Beyond the Dudikoff statue, there was in fact another stage, shrouded by a thick purple curtain.

"What the—" Nick began.

"Ladies and gentlemen," Mayor Doug said, "please give a big Turbo City welcome to C+C Music Factory."

The curtain slid aside.

Bass boomed.

Nick's jaw hit the floor.

For the next three and a half minutes, every last Turbosian ROCKED THE FUCK OUT.

And if Nick or Kanna had bothered to look up, they might have noticed a cloud that strangely recalled Master Kikuchi's weathered visage.

Smiling down on them all.

THE FUCK ELSE CAN I SAY?

AT A NEWSPAPER kiosk outside Nick's apartment, a well-weathered man bent down to check out the day's headlines.

LOCAL NINJA SAVES CITY, the paper said.

The man nodded to himself, turned on his busted heels, and walked off down the street.

"Now THAT'S a fuckin' headline."

THE END

CURSE OF THE NINJA

LUCAS MANGUM

SOMEWHERE IN SUBURBIA. 1991.

FATHER DOUGLAS BRINGS his Camry to a stop in front of the Straker residence. Father William clutches the bag in his lap, praying he remembered everything. Two crucifixes. Several vials of holy water. A Bible. His lucky uniform.

"You ready?" Father Douglas asks. The much older priest cocks an eyebrow at his young protégé.

"Yeah."

"You sure? Performing an exorcism is nothing like shoot fighting."

"I'm aware, and I'm ready, Father."

Douglas eyes him for another beat, then nods. "All right," he says. "Let's go."

They step out of the car and walk up the stone path to the Straker's front door. Father Douglas rings the doorbell. Mrs. Straker answers the door, looking like she hasn't slept in ten years. Her eyes are shadowed. Her hair is a matted mess. The corners of her mouth sag like someone's tied invisible weights to them. It's a shame, William thinks. She was probably a beautiful woman once, but having a child possessed by a demon must add decades to one's life. It can't be easy at all, and William feels for her.

"Where's the boy?" Father Douglas says.

"Upstairs in his room," she says.

"Sleeping?" William asks.

Mrs. Straker fixes him with her weary gaze.

"He never sleeps anymore."

"I'm sorry, ma'am."

She turns back to Father Douglas.

"Please save my boy," she says.

"We'll do our best."

She steps aside and lets the two priests enter the home. A voice booms from upstairs as soon as the door closes behind them.

"MOTHER, YOU DIRTY WHORE! LOOKING FOR SOME DOUBLE-PENETRATION FROM MEN OF THE CLOTH WHILE DADDY'S AWAY?"

Mrs. Straker looks down and sighs. Pink blooms in her cheeks.

"I'm sorry," she says.

"It's not your fault," Father William says.

Father Douglas fixes him with an icy glare that says, *of course it's the mother's fault. The atheist bitch raised this boy in a godless home. What did she expect to happen? She's only called us because she doesn't know what else to do. Even if we save her boy, she'll become no more than a Christmas and Easter Christian at best.*

Father William looks away from his mentor's judgmental gaze and heads for the stairwell. The demon laughs like a witch from a kid's cartoon, all high pitched and filled with long *E* sounds.

"*YOU WICKED BITCH, MOTHER! YOU'RE GOING TO LET THEM HAVE A GO AT ME FIRST? LIKE I'M SOME HELPLESS ALTAR BOY?*"

Behind Father William, the boy's mother begins to cry. Father Douglas pushes past him, taking the steps three at a time. William maintains a deliberate pace.

When they reach the upstairs loft, it isn't difficult to see which room the boy is in. The door is ajar. Vomit green mist billows through the crack. The demon's laughter has turned guttural.

"Come and get me, priests," he says, his voice now a raspy whisper.

The priests enter the room. The mist clears. The boy levitates above the bed in a lotus position with his eyes closed. He looks peaceful.

Father Douglas flashes a look at William, who doesn't like the uncertainty in his mentor's face. He likes the familiar pose of the boy even less. It brings back memories from his old life.

"Hand me the Bible, William," Douglas says. William hands him the Bible. Douglas makes the sign of the cross with it. "In the name of the Father, Son, and Holy Spirit—"

"*AMEN!*" the boy yells and breaks from his position.

He moves quickly, kicking Father Douglas in the face, who grunts and staggers across the room, crashing into a shelf full of Transformers and Ninja Turtles. He falls to his hands and knees, spitting blood and teeth.

Father William meets the gaze of the boy who now stands on the edge of the bed. He does not have the eyes of the boy in the school photo Mrs. Straker presented them. He doesn't have the yellow or black or red eyes of something demonic either.

He has the silver eyes of Father William's old enemy. An enemy thought vanquished. Poe Darrin, master of ninjutsu and violent militant.

A smile twitches on the boy's face, knowing he's been recognized.

Before William can do anything else, Poe cries out again and hits Father Douglas with a devastating ax kick to the back of the neck. William's mentor hits the floor face-first and goes limp.

Poe crosses the boy's arms and stares at William. The knowing smile is more pronounced.

"You know why I've come," the boy speaks in Poe's voice. "We've got a fight to finish, and this was the only way I knew how to draw you back out."

The boy leaps and rears back his fist to hit Douglas with a fatal blow.

William acts fast, hitting the boy with a front kick to the chest. The boy sails across the room and crashes into a framed *Star Wars* poster. Glass shatters and rains to the bed. The frame falls over the boy's shoulders. The poster crumples flaccidly on top of the nightstand.

William grabs Douglas under the arms and hauls him out the door.

Behind them, Poe's voice becomes the demon's again. The high-pitched, long *E* laughter overdubs the guttural, low-pitched chortling as William helps Douglas down the stairs.

"What the fuck was he talking about?" Father Douglas says while holding a frozen steak to his jaw.

Mrs. Straker's eyes widen at the priest's vulgarity.

William sits calmly, hands folded. "I'm afraid that my past has come back to haunt me," he says. He looks at Mrs. Straker. "I'm sorry for the pain this has caused your family. It was cruel of him to involve your son, but my enemy has done this to get at me. It is my responsibility."

"So, my son is not possessed by a demon?"

"Of course he is," Father Douglas says. "The demon is just trying to get to my colleague, and frankly, it sounds like it's working."

"No. If you'd seen what I saw in the boy's eyes, you'd know I am right."

"I'm telling you, William. Your enemy is not inside that boy."

William huffs. He hates to say what he means to say next but knows he must.

"When was the last time a demon kicked your ass like that, Father Douglas?" Father Douglas looks down and says nothing. "Poe Darrin killed my brothers. I thought he died in the fire, too, but apparently, even death could not contain his evil. This is my fight to finish."

Father Douglas groans, but says no more. He either knows William is right or is in too much pain to continue arguing.

Mrs. Straker frowns.

"So, what do you have to do?" she asks.

Father William opens the bag. He roots through the exorcism tools and pulls out a blue shinobi shōzoku. Father Douglas opens his mouth, revealing gaps where his teeth used to be.

"You just had that costume in there the whole time?" he asks.

"Only for luck. I never thought I'd wear it again." He turns to Mrs. Straker. "May I use your bathroom?"

As he changes into his old uniform, William hears the laughter, not the put-on demonic chortling, but that of his old enemy. The sadistic mirth of the man who killed his brothers.

"You're going to die up here, William. You're going to join your family in Hell."

More laughter as William knots his black headband.

He exits the bathroom. Douglas and Mrs. Straker stare at him, wide-eyed.

"You won't . . . hurt my son, will you?" she asks.

"He'll live," William says.

Mrs. Straker steps forward, but Douglas grabs her by the elbow.

"Let him go. This world is beyond both of our understanding."

William gives them a curt nod and heads back upstairs. The boy is back in the lotus position, but his silver eyes are wide and staring. He smirks when he sees William enter. He drifts to the floor, plants his feet in a fighting stance. William matches the pose.

Columns of fire rise from the floor. William shows no fear. He holds the pose and keeps breathing. He never takes his eyes off his adversary, even as the fires rise to nearly six feet. Even as the columns grow arms. Even as their bases split into legs. Even as the fires extinguish, leaving charcoal human figures around the room.

But then the ashes chip away from their faces, and William sees who Poe has summoned. His brothers stand around him. They raise their hands and part their legs in matching fighting stances. Their flesh is gray with death, their eyes white and lifeless. William's resolve wavers and he takes a step back.

His resurrected brothers step toward him. Poe folds the boy's arms and stands there smiling, ready to let the undead do his dirty work.

William closes his eyes and returns to his stance. He doesn't open them right away. Instead, he focuses on the energies in the room. Searches the minds of his brothers.

"YOU LET US DIE, WILLIAM! NOW WE HAVE OUR REVENGE!"

It is not them speaking. He knows this and makes sure Poe knows this. He channels his renewed resolve. Shows it to his opponent. He opens his eyes as his brothers turn on the one who summoned them. Two of them grab the boy by the arms.

"No," Poe says. "You won't let them hurt me. If you do, the boy will die."

William steps forward.

"The power of my fist compels you!"

He punches the boy in the chest. The boy flies back onto the bed, breaking the holds of William's brothers. A white, smoky substance swirls from the mouth of the fallen body. It's not quite human, but within it, William can see Poe's hateful, silver glare.

William steps out with his left foot, raises his right knee, and thrusts forward with a side kick. The blow strikes the cloud, dissipating it into pieces that fly into the resurrected brothers who return to columns of fire and sink into the floor. Gone, now forever.

Father William goes to the boy and checks his pulse. He's alive and free from Poe Darrin's possession. William takes the boy's hand and calls Mrs. Straker upstairs to give her the good news.

"Where will you go now?" Father Douglas asks from the hospital bed a week after the ordeal at the Straker residence.

William stands beside him in plainclothes.

"I will wander the world and help where I can. The world will always need ninjas, whether they know it or not."

Douglas pushes himself to a sitting position, wincing from his injuries.

"And what of the Church?"

"The Church is in me, just as it is in you, Father."

"You speak blasphemy."

William smiles. "If God's got a problem, he knows where to find me. A ninja never backs down from a challenge."

THE END

THIRSTY FOR A NERDY CRIME CAPER?

COMIC CONS

COMING SUMMER 2021!

ACKNOWLEDGEMENTS

There are a couple people I'd like to thank. Myself, of course. Good job, B!

Stephen Graham Jones, Tod Goldberg, and Joshua Malkin, who I'm going to be thanking in most acknowledgements pages.

John Lynch, for reading an early version of this manuscript and providing invaluable feedback.

Max Booth III, for his editing prowess and calling me out for using the word "fuck" over 150 times.

Lori Michelle for the incredibly easy-on-the-eyes layout you just enjoyed.

Matthew Revert, for the super dope cover and interior sketches. Marc Vuletich for the equally rad ad for *Comic Cons*.

My agent, Jennie Dunham.

Lucas Mangum for contributing a kick-ass short story to this volume and a whole bunch of other rad shit.

Michael Dudikoff, Steve James, Bruce Lee, Jackie Chan, Jet Li, Arnold Schwarzenegger, Jean Claude Van Damme, and Steven Seagal, who taught young me how to kick ass. Plus Gareth Evans, Joe Taslim, and Iko Uwais, for teaching older me how to keep doing it.

Also Jon Hurwitz, Hayden Schlossberg, Josh Heald, Ralph Macchio, Martin Kove, William Zabka, and everybody else involved with *Cobra Kai,* for teaching me how to treat the things you dug as a kid with love.

Robert Patrick for inspiring Kundarai Saru via the absolute acting clinic he put on in *Double Dragon* as the villainous Koga Shuko (talk about your Oscar snubs!).

Makoto Kikuchi and the rest of the Data East team for their work on *Bad Dudes vs. DragonNinja.*

Bottle Logic, Green Cheek, Pure Project, the 4th Horseman, and San Diego Tap Room, for keeping me fed and buzzed during the writing of this MS.

All my horror people, on Twitter and IRL.

You, especially, for reading this book, and if you don't mind maybe give it a review on Amazon and Goodreads?

And Jaclyn, for everything, always.

ABOUT THIS DUDE

Brian Asman is a writer and editor from San Diego, CA. He's the author of *I'm Not Even Supposed to Be Here Today* from Eraserhead Press and *Jailbroke* from Mutated Media. He's recently published short stories in the anthologies *Breaking Bizarro, Welcome to the Splatter Club* and *Lost Films*, and comics in *Tales of Horrorgasm*. An anthology he co-edited with Danger Slater, *Boinking Bizarro*, was recently released by Death's Head Press. He holds an MFA from UCR-Palm Desert. He's represented by Dunham Literary, Inc. Max Booth III is his hype man. Find him on Instagram or Twitter (@thebrianasman), Facebook (brian.asman.14), or his website www.brianasmanbooks.com.

Here's a picture he drew of Koga Shuko, the villain of 1994's *Double Dragon*:

(It's Robert Patrick with an Everclear goatee)